CRASH STOP

• MARY GRIGGS •

Bella
BOOKS

2012

Bella Books, Inc.
P.O. Box 10543
Tallahassee, FL 32302

Printed in the United States of America on acid-free paper
First published 2012

Editor: Nene Adams
Cover Designer: Sandy Knowles

ISBN 13: 978-1-59493-308-0

Other Bella Books by Mary Griggs

Unbroken Circle

Dedicated to all who got a second chance.

Acknowledgments

The bones for the story were written during National Novel Writing Month in 2008. The goal of NaNoWriMo (www.nanowrimo.org) is to write a 50,000-word novel in the thirty days of November. I posted my effort on The Athenaeum (http://xenafiction.net/), an archive site that showcases an extensive collection of lesbian fiction. I want to thank the readers who took the time to review and offer constructive criticism, all of which helped me improve the book.

I would like to thank Jennie and Brian Brick and Charlotte Klasson for being my constant supporters and eager readers. I also want to thank Val Brown for reading over the medical sections of the book and being so generous with her advice.

I'm very grateful for my editor, Nene Adams, who pointed out my head hopping and helped close some pesky plot holes. Without her thorough editing this work would not be complete. Of course, any errors that remain are my own, alone.

Everyone at Bella Books has been a pleasure to work with and I really appreciate the marvelous job Sandy Knowles did on the cover design.

Finally, the support of Fran and John Griggs has been crucial. Without them, I would not be the person I am nor would this book have even been possible. I can't thank them enough.

About the Author

After a decade of running bookstores for Borders Books and Music, Mary Griggs turned her attention toward nonprofit management. She co-owns a consulting firm that focuses on non-profits and serves as Deputy Director of Political Affairs for Forum For Equality, an equality organization that protects the rights of lesbian, gay, bisexual, and transgender people in the state of Louisiana. When she is not advocating for social change, she is exploring the food life of New Orleans and finding new things to write about. *http://www.marygriggs.com*

CHAPTER ONE

"I can't believe it's only eight thirty in the morning. Could this day get any worse?" Gail Joiner asked bitterly. Her sulking daughter, part of the reason for the poor start, sat in sullen silence on the seat beside her.

Gripping the steering wheel so tightly her knuckles turned white, Gail said, "Sierra, don't make me tell you again to put on your seat belt."

Today should have been a holiday for them. Unfortunately, Ken Williams, the new vice president of marketing had decided that Gail needed to be part of the strategic planning session he had called. When her usual sitter begged off with a 103° temperature, she was left with no choice but to bring Sierra to work with her.

Her position as human resources director did not usually put her under the authority of the sales and marketing staff, but with a new VP came new ways of doing business. She was trying to resign herself to rolling with the changes until everything settled down again.

She was already late but the car stayed in park in the driveway. With another glance at her pouting daughter in the passenger seat, she stated through clenched teeth, "Final warning. Put your seat belt on."

"I don't want to go."

"I don't particularly care what you want."

"I told you I could stay by myself." Sierra crossed her arms over her chest. "I'm not a baby anymore."

"In a year or two, we can discuss it. However, your behavior so far today is ample illustration of why I can't leave you on your own." With a silent prayer to St. Monica, the patron saint of mothers of fractious children, she watched as her daughter finally complied.

Sierra made a big production of putting on her seat belt, but the quiet click was enough for Gail to put her green Honda CR-V into gear. Pulling into a gap in the stream of cars heading downtown, she tried not to think about how she might be late to her upcoming meeting.

Distractedly, she said, "I thought you liked hanging out with Chet."

"I wanted to sleep in, not hang out with your assistant."

"So did I, sweetheart. But we've gotten used to eating regularly, and that only happens when someone goes to work and brings home a paycheck."

"I don't have to work."

"I'm aware of that. You should realize, though, that someday your blissful little schoolgirl existence will be over and you'll be going to work every morning like the rest of us."

"I'll marry well."

"You'll what?" Gail's horrified screech did nothing to soothe her headache.

"That's what Aunt Elizabeth said. If I marry well, I won't have to work like you."

"So much for all those feminist fairy tales I read to you when you were a child," Gail muttered. She wanted to pull out her red hair by the roots. Instead, she took her eyes off the traffic in front of her to look at herself in the rearview mirror, pleased to note the only sign of the morning's trauma was a small streak of soot across one plump cheek.

She licked her thumb and rubbed at the offending spot on her cheek. Still miffed, she glanced at her daughter. "I can't believe you put the Toaster Scrambles box in the oven."

"How was I supposed to know any better?"

"Maybe if you read the directions instead of just charging full speed ahead, we wouldn't have had flames shooting out of the oven this morning."

"I don't know why you're so mad. You got the fire under control in no time."

"Trust me when I tell you this, sweetie: no fire is a good fire, especially in the oven." She smoothly exited the interstate and navigated the rush hour traffic on the surface streets that led to the port area.

"Nobody died."

"That's not the point, nor is it a given if your current behavior continues." Gail turned off of the Embarcadero. "Oh, joy," she said with forced gaiety. "We're finally here."

Sierra rolled her eyes and looked out the window.

The complex they headed toward consisted of two warehouses and three buildings on Pier 11. Tisane Enterprises was a privately owned herbal tea company currently experiencing a resurgence in sales now that the health effects of tea had been publicly documented. The stylized tea leaf motif on the arch to the employee parking lot and on the ships bringing black, green and white tea from around the world to San Francisco was becoming ubiquitous around the country.

While some of the newer managers wanted to move the headquarters to a tonier address away from the mess and bother of distribution and production, Gail had secretly cheered when the owner stated his preference to stay on the pier. She loved being able to look out over the water from her desk, and did not really begrudge having to travel from building to building in the course of the day as it brought her that much closer to the action.

Parking the car in her assigned spot, Gail turned off the engine and gravely looked at her daughter. "Sierra, I've got an important meeting today. I need to trust that you won't go wandering off on your own."

"I won't, Mom."

"Good. My assistant will be keeping an eye on you. Let him know if you need anything, but I'm sure you brought the necessary pencils and papers. Work on your homework, and if you finish, read a book. I expect you have enough to stay busy."

Sierra shrugged.

"I'm serious here."

Sierra whipped her bright red hair over her shoulder. "I got that. Can we just go?"

"God save me from peevish offspring." Gail exited the car, grabbing her laptop and briefcase from the backseat. She led the way into the building and toward her office on the third floor.

"How long do I have to be here?"

"We'll be able to head home as soon as the meeting is over." Gail smiled as she took a sheaf of phone messages from the receptionist.

"And that will be when?" persisted Sierra.

"I don't know. I'm hoping to be done by lunchtime."

"Can we go to Pier 39 when you're done?"

"What do you want to do down there?"

"Clam chowder and to ride the merry-go-round."

"Okay. It's a date." Gail ushered Sierra into her office, grateful for her daughter's improved mood. She was willing to agree to most anything, including braving one of the city's biggest tourist traps, to keep things moving smoothly. Sitting down, she immediately dialed into her voice mail and booted up her desktop computer. "Set your stuff on the table over there."

"Can't I use your desk?"

"Not while I'm here. You can move over here when the meeting starts, just don't rearrange anything." Gail shook her head and flipped the page in her calendar. "It took me a week to find everything after your last visit."

"You're exaggerating."

"A little, but I'm serious that I need to be able to find things. Don't move my stuff."

"Whatever." Sierra made a face and pulled out her homework. "Can I go online?"

"No."

"Why not?"

"Because they've started monitoring web usage and I don't want to explain how I spent a morning playing games and IMing." She glanced up at a knock on her door. "Hey, Chet. Just the man I wanted to see."

The tall young man grinned, pushing his wire frame glasses back on his nose. "And how is my assistant today?"

"Wearing on my last nerve."

"Now, now. You just get ready for your meeting with the suits and I'll take care of everything else." Chet Embry preened in his own light gray suit, worn with a deep pink shirt and a turquoise patterned tie. The other members of the administrative team called him Sparkalicious for his sartorial splendor.

"You're a dear, sweet man and I don't know what I'd do without you."

"Keep putting me in for bonuses and raises and you'll never have to find out." Chet winked at her and set a binder on the corner of her desk.

"What's this?"

"I got Ken's assistant to give me a copy of everything they're going to talk about today."

"Absolutely fabulous. Now I'll be able to read ahead and plan on repelling his assault."

"Is it going to be bad?"

"I don't know. I've heard rumblings that he wants to reorganize and make our division accountable to his."

"He's a power mad, tin god."

Raising a warning eyebrow, Gail inclined her head toward Sierra. "Little pitchers tend to repeat things at inopportune times," she warned.

Chet mouthed, "Oops."

"No worries. I've got a good reputation and he won't find me folding easily."

"You go, girl," Chet replied, ushering her out of the office.

As she left, Gail called over her shoulder to Sierra, "Obey Chet as you would...no, strike that. Sierra, just obey Chet, period."

"We'll be fine!" Chet shouted after her.

Gail carried her binder into the conference room, pleased to find that she had arrived early enough to have her choice of seats. She was very glad the extra drama this morning had not resulted in tardiness. Setting down her pens and papers in front of a chair that would allow her to look outside, she went over to the credenza to pour herself a cup of tea.

The buffet table was covered in a mix of antique Chinese tea boxes and modern airtight containers. She marveled at the difference between her current choices and those from her previous job. Instead of a few varieties of mass produced tea bags, Tisane provided a vast selection of loose tea. The labels, neatly penned in calligraphy, listed the name, place of origin, and a small review of the flavor and tips for infusing it.

Gail opened a few jars for a sniff before deciding on a three-year-aged Dan Cong from the Feng Huang Shan valley. She poured a small amount of hot water into one of the many Yixing teapots out on the table, emptying it a moment later. She sprinkled some loose leaves into the teapot and poured in water only a little warmer than room temperature. It would take about fifteen minutes for the cold infusion to give her a good flavor.

Smiling, Gail thought back to her first few weeks at the company. She had only reluctantly attended the mandatory tea ceremony class. While she had scoffed in the beginning, she had found she liked the little rituals that the different kinds of tea required.

Before she started with Tisane, she had thought tea was best served iced and sweet. These days, she knew about hot and cold infusions, how different teapots from cast iron to clay to porcelain could give different flavors to the resulting drink, and how best to add milk to hot tea. She had almost laughed the first time she watched the company president warm his spoon in his tea, and then turn it over to pour the milk over the back of the spoon. However funny it looked, she had to admit that doing it that way kept the cold milk from curdling or breaking.

Sighing, Gail carried her warm pot to the conference table and placed the pot next to her binder. She went back for a slice of poppy seed pound cake. She loved the nutty flavor complemented by the delicate aroma and taste of the tea.

As she returned to her place, other participants began wandering into the room. She was surprised to see that Ken had managed to coerce attendees from nearly every division. Ken's group of lackeys set themselves down at the far side of the table.

Nodding and greeting the other participants, she wondered about the amount of wholly unnecessary work this meeting would produce. She glanced at the binder she had received from Chet, noting that the only department not listed as participating was Distribution. She fumed silently about how some people had been able to weasel out of attending.

Gail sat through the introductions of each of the "team" members and added her biography to the mix when her turn came. She schooled her face into polite interest as Ken began to talk about his ideas for the future. After the third mention of sustainability, she made a bingo table on her notebook so she could place a tick mark beside each buzzword he used.

Even with the game, she was barely able to stay awake. Pouring the last of her tea into her cup, she glanced discreetly at her watch, appalled to find that Ken had been talking for over an hour without pause. She made eye contact with the director of technology. Both of them had to smother smiles.

Ken seemed to sense the restlessness from his captive audience. Beaming in hearty camaraderie, he rubbed his hands together and announced, "Okay, people. We are gathered here to brainstorm about the new campaign to put our tea in every home in the world. I want to hear some brilliance!"

Voices shouted out, "New flavors! Tea kiosks in malls!"

"I don't think tea houses will be a really popular destination for Americans on the go," Ken interjected. "But keep going, we need to hear from everyone."

"How about vending machines with bottles of our tea," someone said.

Gail sighed and began doodling on her pad. This was going to be a long day.

CHAPTER TWO

Lily Rush shoved against the large bay door at the entrance to her domain. Standing a hair under six feet, she used her soccer-hardened, athletic build to force the twenty-foot-tall metal doors far enough apart to squeeze her body through. Running her fingers along the interior wall, she finally reached the switch to automatically open the doors the rest of the way.

She looked out at the dock and the two medium-sized tankers that had arrived overnight and were tied up on either side of the pier. The only thing blocking her panoramic, water level view of the San Francisco Bay Bridge and Treasure Island was the small dockmaster's office.

Turning, she looked into the darkness of her warehouse. It was the major staging area for the company. Pallets of packaged tea ready for shipping stood along one side. Incoming supplies were stacked along the other wall.

As Lily walked out of the brilliant sunshine into the darkness toward her office, she inhaled deeply through her nose. While she enjoyed the usual frenetic pace of her distribution director's job, being the only person in the building and surrounded by the rich scent of tea was even better.

Her initial plan had been to take the day off when the new vice president had demanded her presence at his strategy session. After a couple of hours to think about her own personal strategy, she decided to use the holiday to do a long overdue audit instead. By carbon copying the CEO, she had covered her back against any retaliation from Ken Williams and his marketing team.

In her cramped office, she considered turning on her computer and checking her e-mail. Not wanting to get sucked into the abyss of reading and replying when she could be working, she decided to forgo technology in favor of an old-fashioned, hands-on inventory check.

Picking up the printout she'd had the technology department run on Friday, Lily slid a flashlight from the thigh pocket of her black BDUs. With close to a hundred pages of discrepancies to churn through, she headed into the bowels of the building to track down the first item on the list without further delay.

By the time she completed reconciling ten pages, she needed a distraction. Hearing voices, she flicked off her flashlight and walked stealthily over to find out who had come to see her.

"Eep!" squealed the familiar voice of Chet Embry, the executive assistant to the human resources director. "It's kind of scary in here, isn't it?"

Lily could not see who he was talking to, so she moved a little closer.

"Where is everyone?" another voice asked, sounding female and pretty young.

"I don't know. How about we sing something? That will make it seem less dark."

"I'm not a good singer."

"Can you whistle?"

"Yeah."

"Cool. We can do that instead." Chet whistled a few bars.

Lily smiled to herself.

"Do you know that one?" he asked, pausing for breath.

"No. What is it?"

"'Always Look on the Bright Side of Life.' Have you got a better idea for a tune?"

"There's that song from *Mary Poppins* where the birds whistle."

"You mean 'A Spoonful of Sugar'?"

"Yes, that's it."

The two of them began an off-key warbling as they walked deeper into the warehouse, passing within a couple of feet of the pallet Lily stood beside.

Deciding to reveal herself, Lily stepped forward. "What's all that racket?" she demanded, snorting at how high Chet and his young companion jumped and how loudly they screamed.

"Sheesh, you scared her," Chet said, patting the girl's shoulder reassuringly.

"Only her? I swore I could hear two little girls squealing." Lily stepped from the shadows, giving the interlopers a brief smile before she went back to glowering.

"It's okay, Sierra," Chet said. "She's perfectly harmless."

"Harmless? You wound me to the quick!" Lily staggered back comically into one of the pallets, clutching her chest.

The girl with Chet laughed.

"You can take it, you big goof." Chet smiled. "Lily, it's kind of dead in here."

"You're telling me, Chet. All the lucky ones are off for the holiday." She smiled down at the girl. "And who is your shadow?"

"This is Sierra Joiner, Gail's daughter."

"Ah." Lily reached out and shook Sierra's hand. "It's a pleasure to meet you, Sierra. What did you do to deserve having to come to work today?"

"It's a teacher's workday and my sitter is sick."

"I'm sorry to hear that. Has Chet been showing you the sights?"

"Yes, ma'am."

"I've got a favor to ask," Chet said, digging the toe of his brown leather Ferragamo dress shoe into the concrete.

Lily smiled at his bashful routine. "This ought to be good. Go on, name it."

"Could you keep an eye on Sierra for just a moment or two? I've got something to deliver to the boathouse."

Glancing at the large arrivals board hanging by her office, Lily saw the tanker ship, *Wayfarer*, had docked that morning. "Ah, I didn't realize that Johnny was back."

Chet blushed and ducked his head. "Well, would you?"

"Of course. Go on, we'll be fine." She watched the young man almost skip out the door. Shaking her head at the obvious signs of infatuation, she turned to the girl. "What have you been doing so far today?"

"Homework."

"That's boring. Didn't Chet have anything fun for you to do?"

"He let me put some tea in packages and run all the mail through the machine. I liked how it shot through, but picking it all off the floor was a pain." Sierra looked around. "Why is it so dark in here?"

"I figured since I was the only person who was supposed to be here, not turning on the lights would make any visitors think twice."

"Why do you want them thinking twice?"

"Because I don't want them to bother me."

"Am I bothering you?"

"No." Lily cocked her head. "Unless you were trying to bother me."

"Of course not."

"Well, then, that's settled." Lily glanced around. "I've got an idea that will kill some time. You up for it?"

"Sure," Sierra answered. "Anything has got to be better than homework."

"Don't get too enthusiastic. You might break something." Lily raised her eyebrow. "Does your mom know where you are?"

"No. She's in a stupid meeting with a tin god."

Smothering a snort of laughter, Lily fought to school her expression. "Well, we don't want to worry her." She picked up the wall phone's receiver. "Let me just give your mom a call to make sure she knows where you are, and then we'll go and do something a little more fun." She dialed and was transferred to the main conference room. While she waited for Gail Joiner to come to the phone, she filled her pockets with Koosh balls.

Gail answered the call. "Hello?"

"Hey, Gail. It's eleven thirty. Do you know where your kid is?"

"What? Who is this?"

Rolling her eyes at the uptight human resources director's lack of a sense of humor, she answered, "It's Lily Rush. I'm over in Building Five and Chet has left Sierra with me. I just thought you'd like to know."

"Uh, he did?"

"Yeah, it's no problem. I guess he didn't want to risk her going into the water."

"What?"

"He had things to take to the dockmaster's office."

"Oh." Gail still sounded concerned about her child being handed off. "Is it a problem for her to be there?"

"On the contrary, I was afraid we'd be having too much fun to break for lunch."

"It's lunchtime?"

"Time sure flies when you're having fun, doesn't it?" Lily snickered, still pleased she had found a way to avoid the brainstorming session. "We're going to be here for a while."

"Um, thank you for letting me know."

"No problem." Lily hung up, turned to Sierra, and dangled one of the rubber Koosh balls by a single strand of filament. "Okay, that's out of the way. You want to play war?" she asked, tossing the ball to Sierra.

Giggling, Sierra caught the Koosh. "You have toys at work?"

"I'll have you know that these are bona fide management tools!"

"Right...how do you play?"

"Okay." Lily flipped over one of the pages of inventory on her clipboard and quickly sketched out the warehouse. "Here's what we are going to do..." she began.

CHAPTER THREE

Back in the conference room, Gail looked at the phone receiver. She didn't know if she should be more angry at Chet for handing Sierra off, or at Lily for escaping the planning session and being able to have fun while she was forced to suffer. Her head jerked up when she realized Ken was addressing her. "Excuse me?"

"Are you going to come back to the table, Ms. Joiner?"

"Of course, Ken." She smiled at him sweetly. "I was just speaking to the distribution director."

"Oh." He looked flustered that the call was work related. "Well, that's fine, then."

"I'm glad you agree." Gail remained outwardly serene as she walked back to her seat.

Recovering quickly, Ken looked around the conference table and said with false cheer, "Okay, that disruption is a good stopping point. I'm going to let everyone go and check voice mail and e-mail, and I want your butts back in your seats in thirty minutes."

"Only thirty?" groaned several people.

"I'm serious." Ken glared. "If anyone, and I do mean *anyone* is late, I'm going to lock us all in here until we get a plan in place. If you all are good little workers and come back without delay, we'll be able to take regular breaks." He looked around the room at everyone sitting on the edge of their chairs. "Go and be back in thirty!"

Gail fumed, gathering her things together. Her thoughts were in a whirl. What was Chet thinking? What in the world were Sierra and Lily doing in the warehouse?

"Everything okay, Gail?"

Startled, she looked at Ken. Forcing a smile, she replied, "Sure. Why wouldn't it be?"

"You just look a little tense ever since you spoke to Lily."

"Oh, you know how we are." Gail hated that it was common knowledge that the two of them typically bickered whenever they attended the same meeting.

Ken laughed. "You know, I was almost sad when I got the e-mail from her that she wouldn't be making our brainstorming session," he said.

"Really? Why is that?"

"You two are such fun to watch."

Gail tried not to grimace at Ken's expression. "We both feel strongly about our responsibilities to our departments."

"Oh, you don't have to justify yourself to me. I just like to fantasize about what might happen if it went beyond verbal altercations."

"Just stop right there, Ken."

"What?"

"This is bordering on sexual harassment."

"You're kidding me. I haven't done anything!"

"Except make me very uncomfortable with your conjecture about Lily and me," Gail warned. "Those sorts of insinuations about the two of us make the work environment hostile."

"Believe me, babe. None of us was working." Ken winked at her.

"What were we doing?"

He tapped his temple. "In my mind, I was watching you two catfight."

"That's it. I'm going to put you on report."

"Don't you have a sense a humor?" Ken spread his arms wide. "I'm joking here."

"I don't find it funny, and I bet Lily would agree me." Gail grinned at Ken's sudden loss of color. "In fact, I think I'll tell her before I send the paperwork to your boss."

"No, no. There's no need to be nasty." Ken pulled at his necktie. "Look, I'm sorry, okay? It was just a little humor to lighten the mood."

"My mood was fine," Gail lied without blinking. "You knew I didn't find it funny and you kept pushing. That's totally unacceptable, especially from a ranking officer of the company."

"I get that. I'm sorry."

"I'll accept your apology if you promise not to go there again. I don't appreciate the insinuation, and I'm sure Lily would agree with me."

"You don't have to tell her."

"If you control yourself, I won't have to." Gail reflected briefly on the irony of using her rival to threaten a vice president.

"I promise."

"Good. Now, if you don't mind, I've got to go and check my voice mail." Without a backward glance, Gail walked out of the conference room.

As soon as she left Ken's side, her mind went back to thinking about her relationship with the prickly distribution director.

She thought back to their very first meeting, when she had been so happy to start working at Tisane. The job was everything she wanted. She recalled that she had been smiling when the company founder had called out to an approaching woman, but Lily Rush had barely spared her a glance or a word as she pushed past the small group of employees welcoming her.

Since that fateful meeting, they had not gotten along. It seemed like Lily had a negative response to every proposal she made, especially any that involved performance management. Gail knew that things were bad if Ken brought up their turbulent relationship, since he had only been on the job for a couple of months. She cringed that he was privy to any gossip about her.

She worked very hard to keep her private life private. People at work knew about her daughter because she was very proud of Sierra, but other information was off-limits. She did not care if people assumed she was straight or if they thought her cold. She never wanted to be forced to leave another job on account of an office romance falling apart.

Gail snarled at her current predicament. She was stuck at this time-wasting meeting and did not even have the time to check on what was happening with her daughter. She might be many things, but she was not a careless mother.

"I could be mother of the freaking year," Gail muttered, pushing open the stairwell door. She chose to take the stairs to work off some of her bad mood, but the exercise failed to calm her down. Pulling open the door to the third floor, she grumbled, "If anyone thinks I am going to sit back and allow my mothering skills to be maligned, they've got another think coming."

Gail ignored everyone else as she stalked down the window-lined hallway to her office. She decided the minute she got safely behind the closed door, she would give her assistant a talking to that would strip paint from the walls. She would make sure Chet knew that leaving her child with a virtual stranger wasn't acceptable.

Out of the corner of her eye, she noticed an odd movement on the water. Turning her head, she looked out the floor-to-ceiling window.

At first, the view seemed completely normal. San Francisco Bay was filled with a tankers, cruise ships, and a large number of pleasure craft. When she focused on what had captured her attention, her heart began to pound. All the vessels seemed to be moving parallel to the shore except for a large cargo ship headed at high speed directly toward the pier.

Her mouth dropped open when she saw the towering ship slice a thirty-five-foot sailboat in half. Appalled, she continued staring as a tugboat was pushed aside like it was a child's toy.

Gail watched in total disbelief as the massive ship sped toward land, growing larger and larger until it seemed to fill the skyline. Without slowing down, or even giving a warning blow of its horn, the ship plowed into the pier. For a moment, it reared up, showing its great red underbelly before crashing down and tipping onto its side.

A spray of concrete flew into the air as the pilings and Building Five took the brunt of the big ship's weight. The reverberation knocked Gail to her knees. In horror, she stood up to see the warehouse building collapse under the weight of the massive ship. Dust slowly cleared, revealing the ship's enormous propellers still spinning.

Gail heard screaming and it was not until she stopped to draw breath that she realized it was coming from her throat. Frantic, she fought to get clear of the people who had joined her at the window, and tore out of building, running to get as close as she could get to the pile of rubble that used to be a warehouse.

The smells of diesel fuel and seaweed and clouds of concrete dust hung in the air. Some part of her brain was grateful that there was no scent of fire, but she was overwhelmed by the need to find her daughter. She flung herself at the remains of the warehouse and began clawing at the rubble with her bare hands before she was pulled away by several dockworkers.

Trying to fight off the restraining hands, she burst into tears. "Ma'am, what is it?" someone asked her.

"My daughter's in there," Gail gasped. She struggled for a few more minutes, but the burly dockworkers had a good grip on her arms. "Lily called me right before it happened."

"Do you know if anyone else was in there?"

"I don't know! Sierra!" Gail screamed.

"Just wait for the fire and rescue squad to get here."

"Yeah. It isn't safe for you to be pulling things off. It could destabilize this mess even further."

"But my daughter," she wailed.

The men looked at one another. Barry Herren, one of the dock supervisors, finally nodded. "Look. We'll let you go if you promise to stay back."

"But..."

"I'll start my men on moving what they can." Barry waved over his crew. The men picked up crowbars and began shifting the crumbled masonry at the edges of the remains.

Gail stood by, trembling while she watched the men work. She wanted to scream at them, but was afraid they would go even slower. Her vision tunneled until all she saw was the rubble.

"I'm told you know who was in the building?"

Gail turned to face a large, beefy man in a San Francisco Fire Department uniform. The label on his breast pocket read Knight.

She took a calming breath and replied, "I only know about my daughter and the distribution director."

"What was your daughter doing down here?"

"She was going around with Chet. He's my assistant." Gail frowned. "I haven't seen him. Is he all right?"

"Do you know where he was?"

"I think he had to deliver something to one of the ships docked on the other side." Gail pointed at the capsized cargo ship. "There were two ships on the other side of that one."

"I'll check on it." The man spoke into the mic of his shoulder radio. "Who else was with her?" he asked, returning his attention to Gail.

"Lily. Lily Rush."

"Do you know where they were in the building?"

"Lily had just called me. There wasn't an echo, so I think it was the phone in her office." She shuddered. "Wait, talk to Chet. She said he had just left, so they probably weren't far from where he saw them last."

"If we're lucky, the walls fell in such a way that there was a pocket of safety."

"My daughter's school does all the earthquake drills. She'd know where to go if there was only time." She started shaking again. "But it happened so fast. There was no warning. The ship just plowed into them. How would they have been able to do anything?"

"Ma'am, hold onto positive thoughts. It took me years to earn these captain's bars and, in that time, I've seen worse exteriors and gotten folks out who had hardly a scratch on them." He turned and continued speaking into his radio.

Gail watched numbly as uniformed rescue workers replaced the dockworkers moving the rubble.

"Oh, God, Gail. I'm so sorry," Chet said, rushing toward her past the officers. A layer of concrete dust darkened his light brown skin. Tears made muddy tracks down his face.

"Chet, tell them where you saw Sierra last!" she demanded.

"By her office. It's in the back corner."

"Was anyone else there?"

"No. The place was a tomb." Chet's hand flew to cover his mouth. "Oh, God, I didn't mean anything by it."

"Don't worry about it. The information you've given us is good. I'll tell my people to begin their search there." Captain Knight nodded at the EMT standing next to them.

Gail hardly noticed when a blanket was put over her shoulders. She absently took the cup of hot tea offered by a co-worker while never taking her eyes off the pile of rubble standing between her and her baby. When the EMT tried to get between her and the view, she dodged the helpful hands.

"Just leave me alone," she spat.

"Ma'am, I just want to make sure that you're all right." The young woman gave her a sympathetic look.

Shaking her head, Gail said, "I won't be all right until my daughter is found."

CHAPTER FOUR

Lily opened up her eyes and wondered how night had fallen so quickly. She blinked a few times, trying to remember where the day had gone. Slowly, her eyes adjusted and she began to make out shadows in the darkness. Piles of jagged things and looming shapes surrounded her. When she tried to shift her body to see more, she nearly cried out in pain.

Focusing on her breathing, she took stock of her situation. She lay on her stomach and felt a great weight on her back pinning her down. Her left arm was trapped underneath her, too numb to feel if she was actually wiggling her fingers. Her other arm was stretched out and hurt from her collarbone to her wrist.

She coughed, and then wished fervently that she hadn't. It felt like her chest was squeezed in a vise.

"Hey? Are you there?"

Lily blinked again at the whispered words in a young girl's voice. "Hello," she croaked.

"Are you...uh...alive?"

"I think so." Lily suddenly remembered why her arm was outstretched. She had seen the wall collapsing and shoved the girl under the worktable. "Um, I can't remember your name."

"Sierra. Do you think it was an earthquake?"

"No," Lily said emphatically. "I don't entirely remember everything leading up to now, but I do know the ground wasn't shaking. The walls just fell down."

"How does that happen?"

"No idea." Lily coughed again and tried to move, worried that she could not feel anything past the agony in the middle of her back. Thinking beyond her own injuries, she asked, "Are you hurt?"

"I don't think so."

"You should check."

"How?"

"Can you move at all?"

"A little."

"Try and feel over your whole body." Lily closed her eyes and concentrated on not coughing. Dust filled her mouth and coated her throat.

"Okay."

Lily blinked. "Okay, what?"

"I'm okay."

"That's very good." Lily thought for a moment. "Describe to me the space you're in."

"I'm under the table."

"Did it collapse any?"

"Yeah. It's sort of slanted down. I'm in a sort of triangle with my back against the wall."

"Do you see or can you feel any metal under there with you?"

"The table legs are metal."

"Okay. Can you find another piece of metal that is loose that you can pick up?"

"Why?"

"It will help those looking for us."

"They are looking, right?"

"Of course. I bet your mom is one of the main lookers."

"You think she's mad?"

"I think she's scared and that she's praying really, really hard for us to get out soon."

Sierra fell silent for a few minutes. Lily rested her eyes. Her body was a throbbing mass of pain.

"Are you scared?"

Lily worked moisture around her mouth before she could croak out an affirmative.

"Me, too." Sierra's voice was small.

Lily would have hit herself if she'd had a hand free to do so. She could not believe it had not occurred to her to reassure the girl. "Sweetie, there is nothing wrong with being scared."

"There isn't?"

"No. I'm frightened half to death."

"But you don't act like it."

"What do you mean?"

"You're thinking about stuff," Sierra sniffed. "I just want my mom."

"Your mom is out there now, wanting you, too. There is nothing wrong with that. You're being very brave."

"I don't feel brave."

"Being brave doesn't mean not feeling fear. It means doing things despite the fear."

"I peed myself."

"So did I."

"Really?"

"Yeah," Lily replied. "And I promise not to tell anyone about you, if you promise not to tell on me."

"Okay."

Once again, silence fell. Lily heard water lapping beneath them and the creaking of stressed metal everywhere around them.

Sierra finally sighed and said, "I don't hear anybody."

"They are just being careful."

"Are you sure they're looking for us? For all we know, the whole city was destroyed."

"I don't think so."

"Why?"

"I remember the wall over there falling inward."

"So?"

"I think whatever happened came from the water. The only things on the water are ships."

"A boat did this?"

"Maybe a really big ass one."

"How?" Sierra seemed confused. "Why?"

"It could have lost control and crashed." Lily shrugged and nearly screamed when her back spasmed. She heard Sierra calling to her, but did not have enough air to breathe, much less speak.

Slowly, the clenched muscles in her back relaxed. Her head dropped back to the floor. "Oh, fuck me," she groaned.

"You said a real bad word."

"Sorry. I'll wash my mouth out with soap once we get out of here."

"When will that be?"

"No idea."

"But we are going to get out, right?"

Taking as deep a breath as she could, Lily released it a little at a time. "We are going to get out of here, Sierra," she stated.

"When?" Sierra demanded.

"I don't know when but I do know they will get us out."

"What's taking so long?"

"They have to move slowly." Lily stifled a groan. "If they rush, they could make things worse, not better." She listened for sounds of rescue when Sierra stopped speaking. After few moments, she tried to shift position and had to bite back another curse.

"Hey, Sierra?"

"Yeah?"

"Have you been able to look for something to beat against the metal table legs?"

"I didn't look."

Closing her eyes, Lily listened to the sounds of Sierra scrabbling around before she heard a tiny tapping. She smiled at the small noise. "What are you using?"

"A binder clip."

"Try and find something bigger and hit the leg harder. Do it in sets of three. We need to make sure they can hear us through all this concrete."

"Why three?"

"Once could be a fluke, twice could be natural, but three hits would definitely be made by a survivor."

The rhythmic sound of Sierra tapping beat in time with the throbbing in Lily's skull. Closing her eyes, she soon started to drift off. She was startled awake when Sierra spoke up.

"I'm bored!"

"Don't give up."

"But I'm bored."

"How about we play a game?"

"What kind of game can we play trapped like this?"

"Word games."

"That doesn't sound like fun."

"Your choice. Tapping and playing a game or tapping quietly."

"Tell me about the game."

"Um," Lily thought. "Well, since you're tapping in threes, why don't we think of other sets of three?"

"Like what?"

"Three little pigs, or Goldilocks and the three bears."

"Three blind mice!"

"Good," Lily praised. "Keep tapping. I say the Three Stooges."

"Harry, Hermione, and Ron from Harry Potter."

"All right. Three branches of government. Executive, judicial and legislative."

"Hat trick."

"Oh, that's excellent." Lily wracked her brain. "Columbus had three ships, right?"

"Yeah, the *Niña*, the *Pinta*, and the *Santa Maria*." Sierra tapped several sets.

"Need help?" Lily asked.

"No, I'll think of another." After silently completing several more sets of taps, Sierra shouted, "Three Musketeers!"

"Can you name them?"

"You didn't name the Three Stooges."

"Larry, Moe and Curly."

"Right. I don't know the Musketeers, though."

"Me neither. Do you know the three parts of an atom?"

"We haven't studied them yet."

"Oh. Atoms have protons, neutrons and electrons."

"Primary colors are red, blue and green."

"Nice," Lily answered. She tried to lick her lips, but her mouth was dry. She closed her eyes for just a moment.

"Lily?"

Jerking awake, a new wave of pain shivered down her spine. "Sorry, Sierra. Um, how about rock, paper, scissors?"

"That works. Snap, Crackle, Pop."

"Huh?"

"The Rice Krispies guys."

"I'll have to take your word for it." As Lily tried to come up with another group, she heard three loud bangs from above. "Father, Son and Holy Ghost," she breathed.

"What was that?" Sierra asked.

"They heard you. Knock again. Quickly," Lily cried.

Sierra complied.

Lily nearly sobbed when a triple rap answered. "Thank God," she whispered and rested her throbbing head on the hard concrete floor, trying not to cry. With her arms trapped, she hated to think what would happen when she needed to blow her nose.

"Mom," Sierra yelled.

"You see her?" asked Lily.

"No." Sierra sniffed. "I just want her."

"I know. I hate my mom. Even so, I want her now."

"You really hate her?" Sierra kept tapping. "I say I hate my mom a lot, but I don't mean it."

"Well, I don't really hate mine, either." Lily coughed and tasted blood in her mouth. "I'm angry with her and I haven't spoken to her in a while, though."

"What did she do?"

"It's hard to explain."

"I'm not a baby."

"I know that. I don't think there is anyone else I'd rather be trapped under a building with."

"Really?"

"You bet. You've been a real trouper."

Sierra giggled. "So? Tell me about your mom."

Mentally cursing that the young girl was not easily distracted, Lily replied, "We had a big fight, and things were said that can never be taken back."

"How long ago was that?"

"I was seventeen."

"You haven't seen your parents in forever!"

"Hey! I'm not that old." Lily laughed and coughed. When she regained her breath, she said, "But you're right, it has been a while. Almost twenty years."

"That's sad." Sierra stopped tapping. "Who said it?"

"Huh?"

"You know, whatever it was you fought about. Was it something you said or something she said?"

"She was there when my dad called me something and disowned me. She didn't say a word against him or stick up for me. Later, she said the same thing herself."

"Why are you mad at her and not him?"

"Oh, I was plenty mad at him, but I found out a couple years ago that he died slowly of cancer. His suffering made it easier to forgive him."

Sierra scraped the metal bar on the floor before she spoke again. "Sometimes you can't say something, even if you wanted to, even if saying it would be the right thing to do."

"What are you talking about?" Lily wished she could shift, or move, or anything to get away from this conversation. Not only was she in massive amounts of pain, she was also getting her head shrunk by an eleven-year-old girl.

"I'm just saying. When all the boys called Jeremy a sissy queer, I know I should have said something to them or to a teacher. I didn't do anything, though."

"Peer pressure can be tough."

"It was more than that. I was scared."

"You're saying my mom was too scared to say something?" Lily scoffed. "She was my mother. She should be held to a higher standard."

"Jeremy was my friend. Friends don't let their friends hang out to dry."

"Why did you? I mean, what was the worst that could have happened to you if you had stood up to them?"

"The boys could get mad at me and people could start saying things about me."

"Like what?"

"Like I'm a dyke."

"Is that so wrong?" Lily grinned. "I'm a dyke."

"So's my mom."

Lily lifted her head in surprise and bit back a cry at the pain the movement caused. "Really?" she gasped. "I didn't know that."

"Yeah. And I know it isn't bad, but words hurt, and I don't want to be more of an outcast than I already am." Sierra sighed. "At my last school, hardly anyone would talk to me after Mom came out to the nurse when she wanted Keller to be able to pick me up."

"Who's Keller? A girlfriend?" Lily asked.

"They've broken up since then."

"Oh," Lily murmured. She thought back to her own experiences. High school had been horrible, but she did not remember many elementary school bullies. "Is school really that bad?"

"Not all the time. I have friends and I have my teammates, but I'm not popular or anything."

"Teammates?"

"I play soccer."

"Cool, so do I."

"Really?"

Lily decided not to take offense at the incredulity in Sierra's voice. "I started playing when I was younger than you. It was another thing my mom and I fought about."

"Why? My mom likes me to play. She says that's the only way I'll temper my barbarian impulses and get comfortable in my body."

"Your mom is a smart woman."

"Yeah, she's okay." Sierra paused. In a softer voice, she asked, "How could you go so long without speaking to yours?"

"I left home after the argument. My dad was forcing me to choose between staying at home and living a lie, or leaving and being all alone in the world."

"But you're not alone now."

"I'm not?"

"Of course not. You have me."

Whatever Lily was going to say was lost when a terrible screech sounded above their heads. Suddenly, light and dust poured down as part of the roof covering their refuge was removed. Lily automatically tried to look upward. The resulting pain grayed out her vision and stole her consciousness.

CHAPTER FIVE

The hours passed in slow motion for Gail. She dully watched the rescue workers form a human chain to methodically move smaller pieces of debris hand over hand. Although the company's crane was now underwater, they had been able to drive a forklift onto the pier to drag the larger sections out of the way, each removal carefully braced and supported so the danger of further collapse was reduced.

Every so often, all work halted. The firefighters shut down everything to listen for any sounds from within the collapsed structure. Gail's heart stopped with the work, and she desperately strained her ears for the slightest hint of noise from her child.

At some point, someone brought a chair out for her. She sat perched on the edge of the seat, unable to recall the last time she had prayed, but she was doing so now. She pleaded to every remembered saint from her confirmation classes for her daughter to be all right.

She was glad Chet had found a place to sit behind her. She could hardly bear to look at his anguished face while they continued to wait on the periphery of the rescue effort. It took all her strength not to berate him for bringing her daughter into harm's way.

"I'm so sorry," Chet said after a long silence.

Tonelessly, she replied, "You couldn't have known."

"But she wouldn't have been down here if it hadn't been for me."

"Chet, I really can't say or do anything right now that is going to make you feel better. Okay? I don't blame you." Gail took a deep breath and pinched the bridge of her nose.

"I blame me."

"I don't care about blame or finding fault. I just want my baby back."

"I know. I'm sorry."

Gail turned at the beeping sound of a dump truck backing up. She watched another load of concrete crashing into the container. She only switched her attention back to the recovery effort once the dump truck drove away.

"How could this happen?" she asked.

"I heard the cops say that the captain was unconscious."

"Why didn't someone on board stop the boat?"

"No idea. Container ships are hard to turn because they're so heavy and big."

Gail bit her lip. "There is something I want to know."

"What?"

"I would like to know why you left Sierra with Lily."

"I thought she'd get into less trouble in the warehouse than if I took her down to the ships. I had mail for one of the captains." He leaned forward to peer into her eyes. "Johnny was still on board, too."

"Ah, now I get it." Gail felt too emotionally exhausted to muster any anger. "Your boyfriend came back so you abandoned my girl."

"It wasn't like that at all."

"Really?"

"I admit, I knew I would be distracted by him, but I was thinking about what was best for Sierra before I even knew the ship had arrived."

Gail rubbed her tired eyes. "You're probably right. Water and Sierra could have been a dangerous combination, but why Lily? You know she doesn't like me."

"I don't think that's true."

Raising her eyebrow, Gail stared at him.

"Don't glare at me. I don't know why the two of you fuss so much."

"We can't stand each other."

"Well, I like you both, and I happen to know you're more alike than you think."

"I'm nothing like her."

"Yes, you are."

"No, I'm not."

"You are." Chet smiled for the first time in hours. "In fact, I could name several similarities."

"Whatever."

"No, I'm serious."

"I don't want to hear it." Gail gritted her teeth. "I can't have this conversation now."

"We should have it sometime, though."

"Why?"

"Because I think you two would have been friends had you not gotten off on the wrong foot."

"None of that matters."

"It does."

"Chet," Gail warned.

"No, let me finish. You don't like her, so you doubt she would do everything she could to make sure Sierra was safe."

"Why should she? She doesn't even have kids. Why should she care?"

"Not having kids doesn't disqualify someone from making the right decision."

"But if you add that to her dislike of me…" Gail's voice trailed off.

"Are you kidding? Lily would never let her personal feelings impact her actions."

"So you admit she's got personal feelings."

Chet tightened his lips and looked away. "Not the way you think."

"Whatever." Gail shook her head. "I just want my daughter safe."

"I bet Lily did all she could to ensure that."

"She'd better have," Gail replied ominously. The very idea that Lily might sacrifice Sierra because of their animosity made her stomach churn. She waved away another cup of warm sweetened tea offered by one of her co-workers and went back to praying.

As if in immediate answer to her prayer, she saw several rescue workers hurry over to one of the sections. It looked like they were headed to an area above the corner of the warehouse where Lily's office had been located.

The blanket wrapped around her shoulders slipped to the ground when Gail stood and whispered, "Please."

Suddenly, a shout rang out. The shoulder radios on the firefighters near her crackled to life with the news that they had made contact with survivors.

Gail grabbed a passing rescue worker. "Tell me!" she demanded. "What do you know?"

"The guys on the top of the pile heard some tapping. They tapped back and got an answer." The man grinned at her and squeezed her hand. "Keep the faith. Somebody is alive under there."

Gail nodded and released him to continue on his way. Unable to sit down, she paced back and forth, watching the rescue workers' slow but steady progress.

Soon, she heard another shout followed by cheers. Captain Knight came over to her side. "Ma'am, they've broken through. Both of them are alive."

Gail burst into tears and grabbed the startled firefighter in a hug. He patted her back awkwardly until she released him, and then escaped back to the excavation. Tears made tracks down her cheeks. She fell into Chet's arms, both of them weeping in joy and relief.

"Thank you. Thank you." Gail repeated the words over and over, directing them to God, the rescue workers, and everyone else within earshot. "They are alive," were the sweetest words she had ever heard.

The next hour proved even more excruciating than the previous time she'd spent waiting. Work on the pile of rubble came to a near standstill.

"What's taking so long?" she finally snapped.

One of the firefighters patted her on the shoulder. "They have to be extra careful now."

An EMT nodded. "Yeah, rushing now could undo everything. They're working as fast as they can without making things worse."

"I just want her out of there."

"We know. You'll have her back in your arms soon."

"Not soon enough," Gail replied. She blinked in shock when she saw the firefighters lift a small body with auburn hair from the wreckage. "Oh, my God."

Her heart in her mouth, she watched her daughter passed from one worker to the next until Sierra reached the base of the pile where she was handed off to a paramedic who began to jog her over to the first-aid station.

"Sierra?" she called. "Are you all right, baby?"

Her daughter raised a grubby hand toward her. "Mommy."

Gail could hardly contain herself while the EMTs checked Sierra for injuries, but other than some scratches, she seemed to be perfectly fine and in good spirits. Getting a nod from the older paramedic, she grabbed Sierra in a tight hug.

"Oh, God, baby. I was so worried."

"I was pretty scared, too. Lily said it was okay to be scared, but to keep tapping."

"You were the one doing that?" Captain Knight asked.

"Yeah. She couldn't move so she asked me to be brave and do it."

"We found you faster because of it. You showed great courage."

Sierra blushed and nestled deeper into Gail's arms. "I'm tired."

"I bet you are." Captain Knight smiled. "You should go to the hospital to be completely checked out, but you'll be able to sleep in your own bed tonight."

"Thank you. Thank you all," Gail said. She watched the man return to supervising the operation, and then glanced down at Sierra. "I'm so sorry you had to go through that."

"I'm okay, Mom." Sierra gripped her arm and whispered, "I had an accident, though."

"I'm sure we can get you changed as soon as they check you out." Gail laid her cheek against Sierra's head. "Can you tell me what happened?"

"I'm still not really sure." Sierra looked at the overturned ship with wide eyes. "Lily thought it was a ship."

"Did she?"

"Yeah. She didn't think it was an earthquake."

"She's pretty smart."

"Yeah, I was lucky Lily was there."

"Oh?"

"Yeah. When the walls came down, she pushed me under the table."

"She did?" Gail was a little surprised. "I'm so glad she did and that you're okay."

"Mom?"

"Yes, baby?"

"What does it mean to crash?"

Furrowing her brow at the non sequitur, Gail said, "You've seen car wrecks before."

"No. I mean when people crash."

Gail glanced at the EMT before turning to her daughter. "Where did you hear that?"

"Lily said it to the guys who were helping us get out."

"What exactly did she say?"

"She said for them to get me out first because she was going to crash. She said that I had been trauma…traumatized enough."

Gail turned a shocked look on the paramedic and got a shrug in return.

"Uh, sweetheart," Gail said, "when someone is hurt, the body works to keep it alive. Sometimes when the person is helped, the body can't make an adjustment to the new situation and a person's heart can stop."

"She's going to die?" Sierra tried to wiggle off the gurney.

Gail grabbed her arm. "No! No, she was just warning them so they could be prepared. These people are experts at getting people out of danger."

"But she saved me."

"I know, honey. She'll be okay." Gail said a quick prayer that her words would come true. She needed to thank Lily, and did not know what she or her daughter would do if Lily died.

"You've had quite the day," Gail went on. "Let's go to the hospital now."

"But I want to wait. Lily would wait for me."

Gail shook her head. "We don't know how long that will be. You did say she wanted you to be taken care of."

"But…"

"You need to go to the hospital. I have to know that you're all right. We can check in from there."

"Fine." Clearly exhausted from her ordeal, Sierra let herself be led to the parking lot.

Gail kept an arm around her daughter's shoulder while they walked to the car, so glad to touch her again. She smiled at everyone they passed on their way to the parking area. She felt so happy that her daughter was safe, she was amazed her feet even touched the ground.

Inside the car, as she clicked her seat belt closed, she glanced around. This side of the building on the far side from the dock looked entirely normal except for six news trucks with their satellite dishes extended. It was almost impossible to believe a 120,000-ton ship had beached just a couple of hundred yards away on top of a warehouse that could have easily become a tomb.

She and Sierra waved at the reporters and the police officers holding back the traffic. Making a right turn onto the street, she drove directly to the nearest hospital.

Due to the intense amount of publicity the accident had already garnered, Sierra was seen almost immediately at the Mt. Zion campus of the UCSF Medical Center. The nurses and residents cooed over her and gave her a good scrubbing with antibacterial soap. Redressed in a set of scrubs, she was quickly examined by one of the physicians.

"She might have some bruises and stiffness, but there is

nothing else wrong with her," the doctor reported. "We saw the news and it is a damned miracle."

"I know!" Gail hugged Sierra. "I'm so grateful she's okay."

"She might have nightmares, though. Make sure you schedule some appointments with a mental health professional."

"That's a terrific idea. I can't imagine what it must have been like."

"It was pretty dark," Sierra whispered. "I was under the table and could only see weird shadows."

"Oh, sweetie. We'll keep the light on in your bedroom tonight if you want."

"Okay. Do you know how Lily is?"

"Let me check." Gail called one of the supervisors whom she knew was still at the dock. Unfortunately, Darrell Jones could give her no new information on the rescue effort.

"Nothing to report," she told Sierra. "How about we go home while we wait for news?"

"Sure."

Gail wasted no time driving them home. She practically pulled Sierra upstairs and into the master bathroom. Turning on the water, she said, "I'm sure you really want a shower." She turned and saw Sierra just standing in the doorway. "What?"

Sierra crossed her arms over her chest and stared. "Well?"

"Well, what?"

"Aren't you going to leave?"

As she hadn't planned on letting Sierra out of her sight for at least several more years, Gail shrugged. "Um…"

"I'm fine, Mom. You heard the doctor."

"I know you're okay. I'm just in hypermother mode."

"Well, stop. When I'm done here, I'll meet you in the kitchen."

"Oh, okay." Gail slowly started for the door. When Sierra started to tap her foot, she threw her hands up in surrender. "All right. I'm going."

She only went as far as the hallway until the water shut off, then hurried downstairs to sit at the dining room table. Glancing up when Sierra came down, she brightly said, "All better?"

"Yeah. There was dust everywhere." Sierra handed over a towel and bent her head.

Gail smothered a smile. It had been years since her daughter had come to get her hair dried. She accepted the towel and began to use it to give Sierra an impromptu scalp massage.

Finished, she gave Sierra a kiss on the forehead. "Are you hungry, honey?"

"I'm thirsty," Sierra replied, finger combing her hair. She sank down in a chair and stuck a finger through a hole in her shirt. She had dressed in her oldest and softest sweatpants and a sleep shirt Gail had bought at a 10,000 Maniacs concert she attended years before she gave birth.

"If you make that hole much bigger, you'll make that thing unwearable."

"Whatever." Sierra yawned, visibly fighting to keep her eyes open.

Gail smiled at the valiant effort Sierra made to stay awake. "How about I heat you up a nice cup of soup?"

"Okay." Sierra slouched against the arm of her chair. "Do you know if Lily is out yet?"

"No. Let me get the soup heating and I'll call in again." Gail quickly opened a can of tomato soup. "Will you want a grilled cheese sandwich to go with your soup?"

"Yeah. That'd be nice."

"Can you get all the makings together?"

"Sure." Sierra went to the refrigerator for the cheese and butter, set them on the counter, and pulled two slices of bread from the loaf. "Did you want a sandwich, too?"

Gail thought a moment. She had eaten nothing since the slice of pound cake at the beginning of the meeting that morning. "I think I should."

"You think you should? What does that mean?"

"My tummy is still upset from all the worrying today. I know I should eat, but I don't know if I can."

"I'm sorry I worried you."

"Oh, sweetie. You did nothing wrong. No one could have possibly known such a horrible thing was going to happen." Gail hugged Sierra tightly. "I'm just so glad you're all right."

"What about Lily? Is she all right?"

"Let me make the call. You stir the soup and prepare for

sandwich making." Gail walked over to her cell phone. She tried several numbers before she found someone still at the site.

When Darrell answered the call, Gail smiled at Sierra and walked out onto the back porch. "Go on," she said.

"I don't know how to say this except baldly."

"Just tell me, Darrell."

"Freeing your little girl made things harder for them to get at Lily."

"She's still in there?"

"Yeah. It doesn't look real positive."

"But they're still working, right?"

"Yeah. Those guys aren't anywhere near quitting. I know they'll get her out. It's just..." he paused.

"The question is whether they'll get her out dead or alive," Gail whispered.

"We've got to keep good thoughts for her now, ma'am." Darrell's voice dropped. "We're all thanking God that Sierra made it out of there unscathed. Now it is time to pray for Lily."

"Oh, I'm praying all right. Lily saved Sierra's life by pushing her to safety. I owe her more than I could ever repay." She sighed. "Will you be staying there?"

"Yeah. Me and the boys will be here until she's out."

"Will you call me?"

"It might be late."

"I don't think I'll be going to sleep anytime soon."

"Nightmares?"

"Not now that my girl is safe, but I've got enough adrenaline in my system to keep me up for a while."

"All right. I'll let you know. Bye."

"Bye." Gail closed the phone and gnawed on the antenna. After taking a couple of deep breaths, she walked back into the house.

"So?" Sierra asked.

Gail put her hand on Sierra's shoulder. "They're still working on getting her out."

"What? Shouldn't she be out by now?"

"They have to move slow to make sure they do everything right."

Sierra started to tremble. "Getting me out first caused problems, didn't it?"

"Those guys are professionals. They wouldn't have done anything to make things worse."

"Are you sure?"

"Yes, baby. Believe me." Gail led Sierra to the table. She quickly finished assembling the late night meal and brought it out, but she and Sierra only picked at the food.

Finally giving up, Gail poured the lukewarm soup in their bowls down the drain and put the nibbled-on sandwiches in the compost bin on the counter before leading Sierra upstairs.

"Can I sleep with you?" Sierra asked.

"Of course." Gail got ready for bed and beckoned her daughter to get under the covers. When she reached for the nightstand light, Sierra hummed anxiously.

"What, honey?" Gail asked.

"You said you'd leave that on."

"You're right. I'm sorry I almost forgot."

"Thank you."

"No problem." Setting a couple of pillows behind her back, Gail patted her lap. "Put your head down here and try to rest."

"Okay, Mom." Sierra inched her way closer. "She's gonna be all right, isn't she?"

"I hope so. I really, really hope so."

Gail ran her fingers through Sierra's hair. The dark red strands felt thick and cool in her hand. Running her finger over the shell of Sierra's ear, she marveled at her fragility. Slowly, as Sierra's breathing evened out, she whispered a prayer of thanks.

Hours later, she was still awake and gently stroking Sierra's back. When the phone at her hip began to vibrate, she nearly jumped off the bed.

Glancing at the clock, she answered, "Hello. Darrell, yes, thank you for calling…no, you hadn't woken me up." Her hand tightened on the phone as she listened. "Oh, thank God. I'm glad you let me know. Thank you and the rest of the guys for all you did today."

Hanging up the phone, she curled protectively around Sierra. Knowing Lily was finally free from the warehouse ruins allowed her to end her vigil and relax enough to fall asleep.

CHAPTER SIX

Gasping, Gail threw the insect buzzing against her waist into the far wall of her bedroom. The crash of her phone splintering on impact brought her wide awake. She looked at the dent in the drywall, groaned, flung off the covers, and got out of bed.

Walking over, she picked up the three largest pieces. "Damn it," she cursed. "How in the hell am I going to know who called me?"

"Mom?"

Gail's head snapped up. She saw Sierra peering at her from the other side of her bed. "I didn't mean to wake you."

"What happened?"

With a laugh, Gail held out the pieces of her phone. "Well, in my dream, I was being attacked by a humongous bug."

"That's not a bug."

"I had it on vibrate."

"Oh." Sierra yawned and stretched. "Do you suppose they were calling you about Lily?"

"I have no way of knowing." Gail cocked her head. "Were you awake when Darrell called me late last night?"

"No. What did he say?"

"They had just pulled her from the ruins and were about to take her to the hospital."

"Do you know how she is?"

"No. I fell asleep after the call."

"Is there someone you can ask?"

Gail dug the SIM card out of one of the larger pieces of her phone. "My entire phone book is on this. I hardly keep any numbers in my head anymore."

"What are you going to do?"

Gail looked at the clock, surprised that it was almost ten o'clock in the morning. She could not recall the last time she had slept so late. "I bet the phone store in the mall is open. How about we go get me a replacement phone and us a late breakfast?"

"Can we go see Lily, too?"

"We'll have to see about that after I call someone and find out how she is." Collecting all the pieces of plastic in her hand, Gail glanced around for something to put them in. "I'm going downstairs to put these in a plastic bag. Are you going to shower before we leave?"

"Yeah." Sierra wiggled a finger around in her ear, removed it, and wrinkled her nose at the concrete dust coating it. "The dust got everywhere. Even though I showered last night, I've still got it in my ears!"

"Okay. You go ahead. Give a shout out when you're done and I'll take mine."

"All right." Sierra climbed out of bed. At the doorway, she turned around. "Um, Mom?"

"Yes, sweetie?"

"Thanks for letting me stay in here with you last night."

Gail crossed the room and gave Sierra a hug. "Can I make a confession to you?"

"What?"

"After yesterday, I needed to be as close to you as I could. I would have happily slept in your bed had you not wanted to sleep in mine."

"But I only have a twin!"

"It would have been a tight fit, but I would have managed."

"Hey, maybe you should get me a bigger bed. You know, in case something like this ever happens again."

"God forbid. I thought I lost you." Gail gave her a final squeeze and pushed her out the door. "Go on with your dirty self. We're burning daylight."

Dragging her feet, Sierra asked, "Does this mean I don't get a bigger bed?"

"Out!" Gail laughed as she put on her robe and carried the fragments of her phone to the kitchen.

Once downstairs, she called her work voice mail from the kitchen phone, finding fifteen messages from her staff and members of the company offering her their prayers when Sierra's fate was unknown, and six messages from well wishers made after her daughter had been pulled out safely. Ken Williams had left a terse demand for her to call him, but she deleted that call without a trace of guilt.

It was the weekend. She was not going to go into the office or even think about working, and there was nothing Ken could say that would change her mind. She was determined not to give him the opportunity and vowed to report him to the company president if he attempted to retaliate against her. She intended to spend as much time as she could with Sierra. If she were lucky, she would get a chance to thank Lily as well.

She and Sierra chatted quite happily on the drive to the mall, Gail marveling at the change from moody almost teenager to this bright and bubbly girl. She did not want to be grateful for the accident, but if that's what it took to bring Sierra back to humanity, she would give credit where credit was due.

The phone store was fairly quiet for a Saturday. Gail walked up to the counter with her little baggie of shards. "Um, my phone isn't working properly. Could you please fix it?" she asked with a straight face.

The salesclerk looked from the bag to her, obviously dismayed by his decision to come to work today. "What happened?"

"I don't know. It just stopped working."

"Yeah," Sierra piped up. "It stopped right after it hit the wall."

Gail nodded vigorously. "You know, she's right. I'm positive that's when it suddenly just stopped."

Weakly, the salesman asked, "It hit the wall?"

"Well, duh!" Sierra replied. "You didn't think we bought it looking like that!"

Gail could not contain herself any longer. She burst into laughter, as did Sierra. The salesman edged away from them.

"No, no," Gail said, waving him back over. "We're here to replace this phone. It met its death at my hands, and I want another one just like it."

"You're not going to throw this one into a wall too?"

"It wasn't my plan to kill this one. Things just happened that made me snap." Gail smiled sweetly. "I'm all better now. Will you be able to transfer all my data?"

"If the card is intact, sure."

Gail held the SIM out. The young man took it and looked up her account information.

"Will you be interested in purchasing replacement insurance with this phone?" he asked.

"No, the last one was just unlucky."

"Unlucky that the wall got in the way," Sierra added with a snicker.

"Or lucky. If the wall hadn't stopped it, it could have flown all the way into the Pashavarti's yard next door."

"It is entirely your choice to decline coverage, of course," the salesman interrupted. He worked quickly to charge her for a new phone, activate it, and transfer her data. "Here you go. Thank you. Come again."

Gail glanced down at her daughter. "You don't think he wants to get rid of us, do you?"

"I think we'd better leave before he calls the cops."

"All right, but only because I'm starving."

They walked to the food court and made their selections. After consuming some very tasty calories, Gail wiped her hands and smiled at Sierra. "What do you want to do now?"

"Can you check on Lily?"

"Of course. Let me check my voice mail first. There might be a message." Gail made the call and typed in her password. When she heard the start of the message, she sent Sierra away to dump their trash in the receptacles.

She listened to Darrell's voice telling her that Lily's heart had stopped when the final piece of rubble pinning her down had been removed. The paramedics intubated and bagged her for transport to a trauma hospital. The next voice mail message, the call that had woken her up that morning, was from one of her good friends who had heard about what happened on the nightly news and wanted to make sure she and Sierra were okay.

Dialing 411, Gail got the number for Methodist Hospital. She was in phone tree hell for a while, being transferred several times before finally reaching a human being who told her that Lily was in stable but critical condition and that nothing more could be told to her over the phone unless she had a password from the family authorizing her to know more. Gail hung up the phone and saw Sierra standing there.

"What's wrong?" Sierra asked.

"She's still alive."

"Can we see her?"

"No. Only family is allowed to see people when they are as hurt as she is."

"What can we do?"

"I think we can start by thanking our lucky stars that you both made it out alive, and to ask for some angels to take of Lily while she recovers."

"She is going to get better, isn't she?"

"I hope so." Gail looked down at her phone. "You know, Paula called to check on us."

"Really?"

"Yeah. She said something about how it made the news."

"The news? Really?"

"Yep. When you go to school on Monday, you'll be a celebrity."

Sierra smiled for a moment, and then her smile faded. "I'd rather Lily get better."

Putting an arm around her, Gail led her out of the mall. "We'll hope you can have both."

After driving home, Gail realized how worried Sierra remained. "How about I leave you at home and I'll go see if I can get any more information at the hospital?"

"Oh, please, yes."

"I need you to promise that you'll stay away from the kitchen except for ready-made things like soda or chips."

"Can I microwave some popcorn?"

"All right, but that's it." Gail kissed Sierra's forehead. "You're looking a little tired still. Why don't you take a nap, and then put in a movie? I'll leave you here on your own if you promise not to turn on the stove."

"Okay." Sierra's eyes lit up. "Hold on. Wait here!"

Gail blinked as Sierra, a little tornado, flew upstairs, crashed around, and came back downstairs holding something. "What's this?"

"It's the teddy that I won at the Stockton State Fair. Can you give it to Lily? It will help her get better."

"That's a good thought. I just don't know if they'll allow it." At Sierra's disappointed look, Gail shrugged. "I'll try, though."

Sometime later, grimacing at the cost of parking at the hospital lot, Gail locked her car and walked into the cold lobby. She stopped at the main desk where she was told about a waiting room upstairs in the intensive care unit.

She rode the elevator, receiving a smile from one of the nurses. When she looked quizzically back, the nurse nodded, indicating the way she clutched Sierra's teddy bear. She blushed and hurried out of the car when the elevator stopped at the right floor.

Her heels clicked on the floor. The area seemed very calm and quiet. Through a glass door she saw a central station surrounded by a number of rooms. The walls facing the corridor were glass, so she could see each patient and all the machinery keeping them alive.

Aghast, she stopped at the door and just stared around the unit.

"May I help you?" a nurse asked through the intercom beside the door.

"Um, yes. I'm here about Lily. Lily Rush. Can you tell me how she is?"

"Are you family?"

"I'm part of her work family."

"I'm sorry, ma'am. Hospital policy is to not release information except as authorized by family members."

"Please," Gail said. "She's in here because…" She swallowed. "Lily saved my daughter's life."

The nurse looked sympathetically at her. "I'm truly sorry. There is a family member in the waiting area. He might be able to give you an update about her condition."

"Oh. Thank you." Gail walked past the soda and snack machines into a very bright waiting room. Two televisions were on with the volume turned low. A number of cushioned chairs stood around the perimeter.

Quickly raking her gaze over the people in the room, she was not too surprised to see the Tisane company founder and chief executive officer, Wan Yanhai, sitting by himself in a corner. Since she started working for Tisane he had become more than her boss and mentor. She hoped his presence here meant that he and Lily were more than boss and employee too.

He wore tuxedo pants, and his bowtie was undone, hanging loosely in front of his misbuttoned shirt. His short cropped dark hair stuck up in all directions, looking like he had spent hours running his hands through it.

"Oh, hello, Wan," she said.

"Hello, Gail. How is Sierra?" Wan spoke with the faintest of accents. Gail knew his family had arrived in San Francisco when he was entering first grade, but he had never completely erased the soft Mandarin cadence from his speech.

"She slept remarkably well last night, although she was really worried about Lily."

"She was most lucky."

"You're telling me. I think she's the luckiest kid alive."

"We were all lucky. On a regular day, the warehouse would have been teeming with people. I can't imagine what would have happened in that case. It is a miracle no one died."

"You're right." Gail sat down beside him. "How is Lily?"

"Alive." He sighed. "What do you know?"

"Only that her heart stopped when they pulled her from the wreckage." At his puzzled expression, she smiled. "Darrell called."

"Oh, he's a real good guy. His team mobilized, and then stayed there until just a few hours ago making sure things were as safe as possible. They are planning to work all day today and Sunday to see if we can get some operations back up by Monday." Wan shook himself. "Sorry, got a little off track there. You probably don't care about that."

"That's quite all right. It's been a long twenty-four hours."

"Yeah. Anyway, about Lily…a massive section of the wall was pressing a roof support against her spine. When the firefighters removed it, her body went into traumatic shock." Wan rubbed his eyes. "She was intubated at the dock and was in emergency surgery for eight hours and never once breathed on her own. As you probably know, she's in critical condition."

"How bad is it?"

"She's covered in bumps and bruises, and compression trauma on her spine. Several ribs were fractured. The blood flow to her legs was diminished for hours, so she could have nerve damage. She might not be able to walk again." Wan sighed. "We won't know the full extent of it until and unless she wakes up."

"Is that in doubt?"

"She's got some swelling of the brain. That is never a good thing but they haven't had to open her skull to relieve the pressure, so it sure could be worse."

"But she will recover, right?"

"Nothing is certain."

Gail felt a chill of foreboding. "You can't be any more positive than that?"

"She's alive, Gail." Wan patted her leg. "She's alive."

Closing her eyes, Gail took a couple of deep breaths. She was only now realizing how important Lily's full recovery was for Sierra and, if she was honest with herself, to her. She sat next to her boss and mentor in companionable silence for a while. She finally stirred when one of the nurses walked swiftly past the doorway and slid a keycard to access the intensive care unit.

"Do you think they do that on purpose?" Wan asked. "You know, walk fast so it looks like they're hurrying to an emergency."

"I think it's more likely they move fast so no one has a chance to stop them and ask questions."

"You could be right," Wan said. "They are really good about falling back on hospital policy."

"Yeah. They told me they only release info as authorized by the family. They said someone from her family was here."

"They meant me. I'm her family of choice, and she is usually my beard when I need a date at functions that I can't get my boyfriend to attend."

"Oh, really?" Gail asked. She blushed slightly when she recalled seeing Lily and Wan attending a black-tie function together and assuming their relationship was the reason for Lily's hire and promotion to her current position.

Wan stroked a finger over his eyelid. "As you can tell, we are not blood relatives. We're bound by bonds much stronger than that."

"Oh?"

"In fact, you and I have that in common."

"What do you mean?"

Giving her a wry smile, Wan replied, "Just as surely as she saved Sierra, she saved me."

"What?" Gail's head reeled at the new revelation.

"You know anything of my history?"

"Not really."

"I got in trouble with a gang in my senior year of high school and was sent to China for the summer to let things cool off. My ancestors are from the Anhui province and distributed their tea across the mainland. My grandfather opened a packaging plant along the Yangtze River, but he focused primarily on moving our family's product domestically. Once I arrived, I figured there was money to be made directly importing our tea to the United States." He leaned back and crossed his legs. "My timing was fortuitous. With all the publicity around the health effects of tea, I went from importing my family's black teas to green and oolong teas from all over Asia and India. My success allowed me to skip college. Instead, I spent those years traveling around and finding places to sell our tea.

"I loved the travel and wining and dining prospective clients. I also engaged in a lot of high-risk behavior like trolling the seedier bars of whatever city I was in looking for tricks." He paused a moment and cracked the knuckles of both hands. "One night in the Castro, my luck ran out. I ran into a bunch of toughs looking to bash some fags. They considered it a bonus to come across one with slanty eyes."

Gail was outraged. "That's terrible. You would think San Francisco would be safe from hate crimes."

"I was really lucky." He relaxed further in the uncomfortable waiting room chair. "Lily was living on the street at the time. She heard the commotion and kept me from an expensive hospital bill and years of plastic surgery."

"I didn't know."

"Not many do. We don't talk about it much." He looked sidelong at her. "I guess you've heard the gossip?"

Gail coughed nervously. "Uh, sort of."

He winked. "Neither of us ever bothers to deny it. It's not like we're not out, but some days, it is easier to show up to industry functions with someone of the opposite sex on your arm. She certainly would have livened up the event I had to attend last night in Portland."

"Oh, is that why you're dressed liked that?"

"Yes, I didn't even find out about the accident until I was already at the reception for nonalcoholic drink distributors. When I received Carla's call, I headed immediately to the airport."

"Ken didn't call you?"

"No, he didn't. I think he was the most senior member of management on the scene yesterday, not counting you and Lily, who were excusably distracted from letting the company president know about the crisis."

"I was so focused on the rescue efforts, I gave no thought to the business."

"Not to worry." Wan squeezed Gail's knee. "I think I shocked you a minute ago."

Gail dropped her gaze to the floor. She felt ashamed about making assumptions about her boss and Lily, and all the new information made her head spin. She spoke about the biggest revelation. "I didn't know you were gay."

"I knew about you."

"What?"

He held up his hands. "Don't get mad. I just serve on a board with Suzanne Fox."

"I see." Gail examined her nails. "Considering what Sue probably said about me, I'm amazed you hired me."

"You're wrong there. She only had good things to say."

"What?" Shaking her head, Gail was flummoxed. "I don't believe that. She was furious with me. Frankly, she had every right to be so."

"Oh, make no mistake. She is still angry with you for moving and terminating her co-parenting rights, but she understands that your first priority is your daughter. She also recognizes that it was her drinking that forced you to make the decision you did."

"That sounds more enlightened than I would expect."

"Therapy can work wonders." Wan smiled. "She's been sober for two years now."

"I didn't expect that." Gail turned slightly in her chair. Carefully not looking directly at her boss, she asked, "What were some of the good things she had to say?"

"Fishing, Ms. Joiner?"

Cursing her fair skin, Gail felt her color rise.

"She was complimentary of your negotiation skills, your ability to get diverse groups to reach an accord, and your facility with employee relations."

"And you took my ex's word for that?"

"Well, she had been your boss at one time."

"There is that." Gail went back to studying her nails.

"She also kept up with your career these past few years. Based on what I heard from your other employers, you've gotten better with age."

"Thank you." Gail fought to keep a smile off her face. She had never thought to hear such compliments from her ex-boss and ex-lover. The news eased some of the anger she had been carrying around in her heart since their breakup. "So, weren't we talking about Lily?"

"I'm more than willing to change the subject, but you did ask."

"Don't remind me."

"I don't want to embarrass you. What were we talking about before this?"

"Your past with Lily. You had just gotten to where she saved you."

"Right. Well, that night, she lived up to her nickname. As soon as she got the cast off her arm, I had Mitch hire her in the stockroom as an entry-level clerk. We were still in the one building then. That fateful night, I found a dear friend and a great employee."

"She seems a little young for the director's job."

"And you don't? You are less than five years older than her." Wan's voice turned frosty.

"I didn't realize we were so close in age."

"That isn't all you have in common." Wan held up his hand when she tried to speak. "But that isn't my point. You shouldn't think for a moment that she hasn't earned every promotion. I generally don't mess with most hiring decisions, and I especially didn't interfere in her advancement in the company. She's smart and a terrific worker. We're lucky to have her."

"She does a great job. I've never heard of her department having any troubles."

"They wouldn't under her watch. She compels people to perform to a higher standard. Part of it is that she doesn't accept anything less for herself and nobody wants to disappoint her." He laughed. "Even me."

"What do you mean?"

"I got lucky with my company and my family's export contacts. Success came almost too easily. I didn't like doing any of the work that running a business took. When she realized how badly behind we were on the paperwork and filings, she joined forces with my secretary, and got on my case to turn me and the company around."

"Carla is a force to be reckoned with."

"On her own, I could ignore her advice as just coming from support staff. When the two of them gang up on me, I have no choice but to do what they say."

"We don't see much of you."

"That's because I followed her advice. I found the best possible people to do the jobs I dislike. The business runs flawlessly, and I get the time to follow my passion of evangelizing to the masses about the benefits of our products instead of hunkering down in the trenches with endless piles of paperwork."

"Is that how I came to be recruited?" Gail had always wondered why Tisane Enterprises headhunted her from her previous company. She'd had no experience in the beverage industry and no knowledge of tea.

"Yes. I hired an executive search team and put in my priorities. You were one of the top candidates. What I heard from those who know you put you over every other candidate in the field. Lily and all the other directors supported your candidacy, and I think you've been a good fit." He winked again. "And you can't tell me this hasn't been your best job ever."

"You're right. I really love my work. It's a challenge, but it's also rewarding."

"See? I'm always right." Wan glanced up at the beckoning nurse. "Excuse me," he added. "It's time for me to see her."

Gail watched the trim Chinese man enter through the glass doors and follow the nurse to Lily's room.

After the door closed behind him, Gail switched her attention to Headline News' scrolling weather report at the bottom of the TV screen. A reporter had just started reporting baseball scores when Wan returned and sat down next to her.

Sighing, he said, "No change."

"How often can you see her?"

"At the top and bottom of every hour. They give me ten minutes with her."

Gail sat quietly with him for a while, listening to the sounds of the hospital and the low murmur of the televisions. Finally, she cleared her throat and asked one of the questions that had been bothering her. "Have you contacted her family?"

"No."

"Why not?"

"Because she wouldn't want them here."

"They are her family."

"Then they shouldn't have thrown her out when she was a teenager."

"I didn't know that." Gail felt tears prickling at the thought of anyone doing something like that to Sierra. "If they're not around, who's making medical decisions for her?"

"I am as her family of choice. I'm her emergency contact and I have a power of attorney. She's made her wishes very clear. I'm following her directives."

"This is insane. I can't believe that her family wouldn't want to be with her now."

"They have had plenty of chances to be a part of her life. Instead, they rejected all overtures. If they don't want her, she doesn't want them."

"I can't imagine such cruelty to any family member, no matter the circumstances."

"Unfortunately, not everyone has an ideal family. Some of us have messy lives and messier relationships."

"I didn't mean..." Gail stammered, nervously. "I...uh...I never meant to offend you."

"Your intentions don't matter when the result is hurt." He stood up. "I'm going downstairs to get some coffee."

"Please, Wan. Wait a second." At his nod, she said, "I'm sorry. What you've told me about your and her background has been eye-opening. I never knew what you had gone through and I didn't mean to insult you or her."

"I know that. It is just hard to bear your judging us when you don't know all the facts."

"I understand that and I'm sorry. Thank you for sharing with me."

"You're welcome. I think it is important for you to know more of the details of her life."

"Really?" Gail anxiously cleared her throat. "Are you sure she'll be okay with that?"

"Are you?"

Gail considered his question. She finally nodded. "Yeah, I want to know more. I had this idea about who she was and why she was that way, but everything that has happened has shown me how wrong I was. I want to know the real person."

"Sometimes it helps us to have our assumptions challenged."

"Challenged, shaken and stirred," Gail ruefully responded.

"All I ask is that you respect the fact that different paths have brought us together in this place and at this time."

"I will."

"Good. Now, I really need to find myself a cup of coffee."

"Hold on," Gail said, looking at her watch. "What happens when your time to visit comes up again?"

He glanced at the nurse's desk. "Do you promise not to do anything to upset her?"

"She saved the most precious thing in the world to me. I don't want to do anything but thank her."

"Lily won't accept it." He ran a hand through his hair. "I know better than most that she thinks there is nothing special about what she does for other people."

"I don't care. If she won't hear it in words, I'll make sure my actions show her how thankful I am."

Wan studied her. "I'm going to put your name on the list of approved visitors. You can go at the top of the hour." He took a step away before turning back to add, "If I hear that you've done anything to impede her recovery, I'll take you off so fast your head will spin."

"Thank you. I'll be good," Gail vowed, grateful that she was going to be able see Lily with her own eyes.

In due course, Gail was allowed into the unit. Her eyes glistened with tears when she looked at Lily's battered body. The woman lay on her side, her bruised left arm on top a pillow. A small frame kept the covers off of her damaged back. Her head was swaddled in bandages, and a number of tubes and wires from several machines trailed from under the sheet.

"You can talk to her," the nurse said, startling Gail.

"Oh." She blinked. "What should I say?"

"Anything that comes to mind. I'm not sure if she can hear or understand, but it is comforting to hear a friendly voice. It might just be the thing to bring her back."

"All right. I'll give it a try." Taking a deep breath, Gail smiled. "Hey, Lily. It's me, Gail. Wan let me take a turn to see if I could do a better job of getting you to wake up." She studied the readouts.

The monitors picked up no changes. "I want to thank you for what you did." She leaned close. "Before yesterday…before I heard how you were with Sierra and before I talked with Wan, I would have said that your actions were out of character. I know now that they weren't and that means I was wrong about you." Gail swallowed to try to move the lump in her throat. "I need to apologize. I was wrong and I'm so sorry."

"It's time."

"You need to wake up, Lily. We've got some serious talking to do."

The nurse let her leave the teddy bear next to Lily. Gail's eyes teared up again as she left the room. Not stopping at the visitor's room, she exited the hospital and sat in her car until she could see clearly enough to drive home.

CHAPTER SEVEN

"Oh, good. I wasn't sure if you were going to show up today or not." Ken Williams stood in the middle of the lobby with his hands on his hips.

Gail wanted very badly to give the vice president of marketing a piece of her mind. She really did not want to deal with him first thing on a Monday morning. Unfortunately, he had obviously been waiting to waylay her as soon as she came into the building.

"Hello, Ken. How are you today?" she asked, as she kept walking toward her office.

"I'm fine. I'm a bit surprised that you're here today."

"Why is that?"

"I just thought you would need some personal time."

"What are you trying to say?"

"Wouldn't most mothers jump at the chance to stay at home with their kids?"

"I don't know what most mothers would do. Only what I do." Gail took her messages from Chet and walked into her office. "Oh, by the way. Sierra's fine."

"Who? Oh, your daughter." He waved his hand. "Of course, I meant to ask about her."

"No, you didn't." Gail straightened the sleeves of her jacket. "She's just a pawn to you."

"That's not true. I called you over the weekend to…uh, to…"

"Yeah, you called all right, but it had very little to do with any concern for Sierra and less for me. In fact, it begs the question: what do you want from me?"

"I want you to make a statement to the press." Ken studied the diplomas and certificates on her wall instead of making eye contact.

"Why?"

"We need to stay ahead of the curve."

"What does that mean?"

"We're in the process of a new launch. We don't want anyone to think this accident has anything to do with us. The last thing we need is our product line coming to mind when people think of drunken idiots piloting ships. Just remember how Exxon fared after the *Valdez*."

"It's hardly the same thing. There aren't any sea creatures covered in crude outside our building and the ship isn't even ours."

"Tell that to the public. And make sure you call for a full and complete investigation."

"Why am I doing this instead of the company president?"

"Oh, Wan is out of town."

"No, he's not. He was at the hospital yesterday with Lily."

Ken looked a little spooked for a moment. "I didn't realize that. Well, from a marketing standpoint, you're a better option anyway."

"Really? Why?"

"Because you were personally impacted by the accident and it makes you sympathetic. Sort of puts a human face on the tragedy. Additionally, you've got the look we need as we go forward."

"What's that?"

He leered. "You're hot. It'll distract the reporters from asking questions and keep the viewers entertained."

"You're a pig," Gail said flatly. "And if you think anything is going to distract a reporter from getting the real story you're seriously mistaken."

"But I'm also a VP. That trumps your director title." The smile on Ken's face never reached his eyes. "Now, go write something, and make sure you run it by my office before you meet with the press."

"Why aren't you doing this?" Gail stared at him. "I would think, with Wan not here, you would want to be the public face of the company."

"My team and I are focused on the launch. I don't need them distracted from that, and I certainly don't need anyone linking me to this tragedy." Ken straightened his tie. "I do have a reputation to maintain. Now, I've scheduled the press conference for ten thirty, so you've about forty minutes to write something and send it to my office for review. I suggest you get started."

Gail was quietly furious when she sat at her computer to prepare a brief statement. As she typed it out, she wished for her old Selectric typewriter. Anyone hearing someone bang the keys on that machine knew when the typist was angry.

The first version of the statement said exactly what she felt. She read it once before deleting it. With the venting out of her system, she was able to hammer out a fairly diplomatic statement in just a few moments.

She read it over one more time, saying the words out loud to make sure the statement scanned properly. "We hope that the Transportation Safety Administration investigates this destructive accident. Because of the holiday, most of our warehouse staff were safely elsewhere. We were very lucky that there was no loss of life. We have one employee recovering in the hospital, and we appreciate your best wishes for her complete recovery."

She sent it off by e-mail for Ken's approval. He returned it with a snarky message for her to tell everyone that her daughter was okay too. She smiled when Chet announced that the reporters were set up in the main conference room and that she had no time for revisions.

Smoothing down her skirt, Gail tried to hide the quaking in her knees as she marched from her office to the podium. Taking a deep breath, she read the statement before looking around the room. The reporters looked back at her with a mixture of sympathy and hunger. After sipping from a bottle of water, she asked if there were any questions.

"Give us the name," called a reporter.

"Yes. Who is in the hospital?" another reporter asked.

"We will not release the name of the injured employee pending notification of the family." Gail glanced at another reporter who had risen from his seat.

"Was your daughter hurt?"

"No. She escaped unharmed thanks to the heroic efforts of the injured employee."

"Both physically and mentally?"

Gail glared at the reporter. "Excuse me?"

"How is she coping with her ordeal?"

"She is a very resilient young woman."

"Are you seeking professional help for her?"

"That is none of your business," snapped Gail, her grip tightening on the edges of the podium.

"Tell us more about the employee!"

"Tell you what? That she saved my daughter's life at significant risk to her own? That she is in critical condition and in a coma that no one knows when or if she will wake from?" Gail bit her lip to keep from saying more. "Were there any questions concerning Tisane Enterprises?"

She ignored the reporters who continued shouting questions at her about Lily and Sierra. Seeing no other hands raised, she forced a smiled to her face. "Thank you for your concern."

Striding out of the conference room, Gail did not slow down until she reached the safety of her office. She closed her door and leaned back against it, shaking like a leaf. The questions had brought to stark relief how close she had come to losing Sierra and how wrong she must have been about Lily. She prayed that she would have a chance to thank Lily for her sacrifice.

As she looked at her full inbox, Gail knew she was still too worried about Lily to get any work done. She took only long enough to put an "out of office" message on her e-mail and voice mail before opening her office door and checking in both directions.

"What's up, boss?" Chet asked.

"I'm going to the hospital to check on Lily."

"Will you be coming back?"

"I don't know." Gail felt close to tears. She could not stop thinking that it could easily have been Sierra in that hospital bed. "I can't be here while she's in there suffering."

"I understand. I'll handle everything I can."

"Thank you, Chet." Gail's throat closed. She could not say anything more.

Chet seemed to understand. He stood and gave her a hug. "Tell her we're messing with her stuff. That should get her back on her feet in no time."

Gail could not help smiling at that. Without another word, she walked to her car. She was so distracted on the short drive to the hospital that she was grateful the traffic was light at midmorning. Her mind kept replaying the collapsing of the warehouse. Even knowing that Sierra and Lily survived could not lessen her visceral response, and she had to wipe away tears with a napkin she found wadded up in the center console. Once she arrived at the hospital and parked in the garage, she quickly made her way to the twelfth floor.

Wan sat in the same chair. He had changed clothes, but his cheeks were unshaven. He glanced at her tiredly when she walked up to him.

"Have you left at all? Or gotten any sleep?" she asked.

"No. I want to stay until she wakes."

"You won't do her any good if you end up here beside her because you didn't take care of yourself."

"She shouldn't be alone."

"She won't be." Gail reached out and squeezed his hand. "I'll be here."

"For how long? You've got a daughter to take care of."

"She's at school, then she's got soccer practice. She won't be home until around seven o'clock tonight." Gail looked at her wristwatch. "It is only eleven now. You go home. Eat something, nap, and then come back this evening after dinner."

"Are you sure?"

"Yes." Gail nodded. "I'm sure that this is right where I want to be. Where I need to be."

Wan sighed. "Okay." When he stood up, he swayed.

"Are you safe to make it home?"

"I'll call Bobby. He'll look out for me." Wan laughed. "I'll make him park the car."

"You don't have off-street parking?"

"No. It is the bane of my existence, but the house is fabulous. You've got to take the chaff with the wheat." Stretching, he smothered a yawn and turned toward the nurse's station. "I'll let them know you're here, and they'll come and get you when it's your time."

"Thanks. You take care of yourself." Gail smiled slightly as her boss stumbled down the hallway. Needing something to do, she picked up an old issue of *Reader's Digest* and flipped through the pages looking for the jokes.

"Ma'am?"

Gail had become engrossed in reading an article about how a small meal of four to five ounces of protein could help her brain create dopamine and norepinephrine. Sticking her finger between the pages, she glanced up at the nurse. "I'm sorry?"

"We're ready for you."

Gail quickly put the magazine aside and followed the nurse into the unit. She gasped when she stepped into Lily's room. The hours since her last visit had allowed bruises to come out in vivid color. The woman on the bed looked like she'd been painted all over by a demented preschooler with a preference for dark purples and blues.

She smiled at the teddy bear underneath Lily's right hand. Sitting down beside the bed, she petted the bear, and then let her fingers trail onto the hot skin on Lily's arm.

"Lily, it is me, Gail. I'm back to spend today with you. Don't worry, I didn't do anything to Wan. Well, I sent him home to get some food and some rest. Did you know he's been here since you were brought in?"

Wiping the unshed tears from her eyes, she said, "Wan loves you a lot, and you would be doing a great thing if you woke up for him when he comes back." She brushed a few strands of hair off Lily's damp forehead. "And for me." No response, but she remained hopeful that her words or her presence would get through to the unconscious woman.

"Sierra is very worried about you. I don't think she really believes me when I say that you are alive. I think she needs to see you to believe that you'll be okay. To be fair, though, seeing hasn't been enough for me. You did a marvelously wonderful thing. I want you to open your eyes so I know you understand me when I tell you how much your sacrifice means to me."

Gail was about to go on when the head beneath her fingers shifted slightly. She leaned forward eagerly. "That's it. Wake up, Lily."

Moving her hand to Lily's shoulder, she felt muscles bunching and releasing, and saw Lily chewing on the tube. "Please wake up," she whispered.

"Is something happening?" asked the nurse, adjusting the drip of intravenous fluid.

"I don't know." Looking at the nurse, she said, "I felt her move."

"She could be waking up."

"Really?"

"Yes, she is only lightly sedated, so she may soon be awake."

"Is she in pain?"

"No, ma'am. This is a fentanyl drip that will control pain without impeding consciousness."

"That seems cruel." Gail pointed at the tube coming out of Lily's mouth. "She looks like she wants it out."

"You'll hear an alarm when she breathes over the vent."

"An alarm?"

"It looks scary but she won't be suffering. Pain, even in an unconscious person can cause further problems, so we'll control her pain as we reduce the sedation."

Gail sighed. "What can I do to help?"

The nurse adjusted the sheet covering Lily. "It will be a difficult thing to witness."

"I'm not squeamish."

"No, although you might find her struggles disturbing."

"I already do." Gail wrung her hands together. "Tell me what I should do."

"Give her what physical and verbal comfort you can. Keep touching and talking to her."

"And she'll wake up?"

"People wake up in their own good time. When her body is ready and her mind is willing, she'll come back to you."

Gail inclined her head. "All right."

"Good. I'm glad to hear it." The nurse moved to the door. "Unfortunately, that's all your time for now."

Like her grandmother used to do when she was sick, Gail kissed her fingertips and pressed them gently to Lily's temple. She left the room and took her usual seat in the waiting room.

She turned slightly so she could look out the window. A small slice of Coit Tower was visible from the nearby Telegraph Hill. While waiting for her next visit with Lily, she thought about another Lillie, Lillie Hitchcock Coit.

Lillie had been a woman ahead of her time who drank, smoked and gambled. Wearing pants and shaving her head, she was unlike most of the women in San Francisco at the turn of the century. Gail laughed to herself, recalling a story that Lillie had rented out a hotel room for a boxing match after being denied entry to a prizefight because she was a woman.

In fact, Gail thought that Lillie and Lily might be a lot alike. They made their own rules and were their own person. Their philosophy of "damn the consequences" could so easily be misconstrued by those who didn't know them and just judged. Like her, she mused.

She thought back to her talk with Wan, and the sleepless nights she had spent analyzing every past interaction between Lily and herself. She'd felt an intense need to reassess almost every one of their exchanges, from their very first meeting to Lily's joking on the phone before the ship crashed into the building. She had taken the purported malice out of the equation, and had been left contemplating a long series of unfortunate misunderstandings.

Gail knew she had to face her culpability in the crossing of their signals. She pinched her bottom lip, wanting to clear the air between the two of them, but the woman needed to be awake for that to happen.

She steeled herself for her next visit and subsequent visits. During each one, Lily seemed to come closer and closer to consciousness. By late afternoon, she was in obvious discomfort when she tried to shift on the bed.

Lying on her side, only half of Lily's face was visible. Gail saw that Lily's brow was furrowed. She stroked the warm skin, pleased to see Lily's forehead smooth out.

She watched the fingers free of the cast twitch and clutch at the stuffed bear. Sliding her hand under Lily's, she clasped it gently. With her other hand, she continued stroking the lines from the tense forehead.

"Lily, it is okay. It is quite safe for you to wake up. If you do, I know they'll give you the best drugs on the planet. Wouldn't that be nice?"

As Gail spoke, Lily calmed down. Suddenly, an alarm began to sound. Frightened, she looked at the nurse.

"Don't worry," the nurse told her. "Remember what I told you earlier? That is just letting us know she is pulling air on her own. That's a very good sign."

"Will you be able to take the tube out of her throat now?"

"She needs to keep making the effort for a while. We'll wean her off the ventilator first and then, if things go well, she should be free of the tube tonight."

"That's wonderful news!" Gail's voice rose. Lily's hand tightened in hers, and the heart monitor showed an increase in beats.

Smiling, the nurse said, "See, she is responding to your voice."

"So, that's a good thing?"

"Most definitely."

Speaking in a whisper, Gail put her lips right against Lily's ear and said, "That's right, keep trying to breathe on your own. Do it and you'll get that awful thing out of your throat."

"Good. Now, we need to let her rest."

After another fingertip kiss, Gail left to keep her vigil in the waiting room. During her final visit of the evening before she had to leave to pick up Sierra from soccer practice, she was shocked to see Lily's eyes flicker open.

Lily looked blankly at her.

"Hey, Lily. I'm so glad you're awake." Gail spoke softly.

Lily's lips moved. Her eyes blinked once before drifting closed.

"Did she wake up?"

Gail looked at the nurse. "I think so. She may be back asleep now, though."

"Good. Keep talking to her. Try and keep her calm. I'll page for the doctor."

"Is her doctor here?"

"She's on duty in the ER downstairs. She'll be here right away."

Gail nervously stroked Lily's forearm. The skin was soft and felt hot under her fingertips. She knew she was supposed to keep talking, but her mind had gone blank. She had been talking all day. Now there was a possibility that Lily could actually hear her, and she couldn't think of a thing to say.

"Hello."

Gail glanced up, seeing a tired-looking black woman wearing a white coat. The woman's skin was dusky with fatigue although her dark eyes were kind.

"Hi," she replied.

"I'm Dr. Thea Patterson."

"Gail Joiner."

"Is our patient awake?"

"She was for a moment."

The night nurse answered. "Her movements were purposeful."

"Excellent. Too much longer spent unconscious and I'd start to get concerned."

"So this is good?"

"So far." Dr. Patterson pulled the covers down, exposing the injuries on Lily's back. She gently put her stethoscope against the oozing wounds to listen to breath sounds. She cocked her head. "Okay. Can you see if she'll come a little closer to the surface?"

Gail could not take her eyes off the deep cuts and scratches on Lily's back. At the doctor's light touch on her arm, she jumped. "Sorry?"

"I asked you if you could wake her up again."

"I don't know what I did the last time. How am I supposed to do it again?"

"Just try. Talk her into opening her eyes. Sometimes a friendly voice is all it takes."

"We're not really—"

Dr. Patterson held up a hand, interrupting her. "Let me change that to a familiar voice. You're obviously someone she knows, unless you are a random stranger with a fetish for the critically injured."

"No, we work together."

"That's fine. Just give it a try. No big deal, but I'd like to see if she'll respond."

"I'll try." Gail took a breath, and reached out to stroke Lily's head. "Hey, Lily. There are some people here who want to see you wake up. Open your eyes, Lily. Come on. Show me your beautiful eyes. Lily, I'm not fooling around. Open your eyes. Now!"

Lily moaned, her eyes fluttering open briefly before slamming shut again. Dr. Patterson moved Gail to the side and peeled back one of Lily's eyelids while murmuring in a soothing tone to calm Lily's increasing agitation.

"Prepare a sedative." Dr. Patterson straightened and stretched her back.

"Is she going to be okay?" Gail asked.

"I'm hopeful. Her pupils are reacting normally. She may have escaped without any permanent brain damage."

"What about the rest?"

"I'm not sure. I'll have neuro down here, but until the spinal swelling goes down, we won't know for certain what her eventual prognosis will be."

"She could be paralyzed?"

"While nothing was broken, there is significant bruising around her lower spine that is compressing the nerves. We need to wait and see." Dr. Patterson made a notation on the chart and spoke to the nurse. "She's done well and she should rest. Give her a small bolus of pain medication and increase the sedation."

Gail spoke up. "But I thought you couldn't sedate her until she was breathing on her own."

"Another few hours will be soon enough to start working her off the vent." Dr. Patterson smiled. "She's got a good friend in you. She'll sleep for at least two hours and more likely four. Why don't you get some rest, and come back and see her at visiting hours tomorrow?"

Gail glanced at her watch. It was six thirty and she knew Wan was out in the waiting room, anxious for some good news. With a last, lingering glance at Lily, who was now sleeping peacefully, she nodded. "All right. I'll come back in the morning."

CHAPTER EIGHT

The brief view she had had of Lily's eyes opening and the memory of Wan's smiling face were enough to give Gail the energy to drive home from the hospital. She stopped on the way for Chinese takeout from the Jade Palace.

Entering the house, she dropped the bags on the kitchen table and handed several folded bills to the sitter. "I'm so glad you're feeling better, Sarah."

"Thanks, Ms. Joiner. I was glad to hear that Sierra was okay."

"Me, too! Thanks for bringing her home from practice."

"It's easy enough with her school on my way home."

Gail picked up the waxed paper bag of egg rolls. "Want one for the road?"

"Sure!" Sarah took one from the bag.

Gail walked her to the door. "I'll let you know tomorrow if I will need you."

"No problem. I'm always glad for the extra bucks."

Returning to the kitchen, Gail grabbed a soda before shouting, "Sierra, I'm home."

In response, she heard pounding feet coming down the stairs. "Where have you been?" Sierra demanded, coming into the kitchen.

Startled, Gail turned toward the spitfire in the doorway. "Excuse me?"

"Where were you?" Sierra crossed her arms over her chest. "I was hungry."

"I stopped off to get carryout."

"Why didn't you call me?"

"I was at the hospital and had my phone off." Gail reached into her purse and turned on her phone. It powered up without any vibration or icon to indicate that a message had arrived. "I'm not seeing that you left anything for me. You know, sweetheart, phones work both ways."

"I expected you to be here when we got home."

"Sometimes I won't be. I do promise I'll do better at calling if I think I might be delayed, though. Is that okay?"

"Yeah, I suppose." Sierra nodded and started pulling food out of the bag. "Did you get sesame chicken? Where are the pot stickers?"

"Yes, and the pots tickers are in there. I placed a double order so I could be sure I'd get at least one or two."

"Mom!"

"It's true. You're a pot sticker hoarder. Good thing I love you anyway." Gail tore a couple of paper towels off the roll and sat down at the kitchen table, pulling the box of steamed rice closer. "I've got some good news."

"What?"

"Lily opened her eyes today." Gail swallowed a bite of rice and plucked a piece of chicken from another container.

"That's wonderful. Did she ask about me? Can I go and see her?"

"Hold your horses. She only just opened her eyes, and then went back to sleep."

"Oh."

"Sweetheart, that is a good sign. She's really badly hurt and it is going to take awhile before she's able to have visitors."

"You get to see her."

"That's because I'm an adult and I've got permission from her best friend in the world." Gail dipped a pot sticker in sauce. "Besides, it is a bit scary to see her hooked up to all those machines. It gave me nightmares after the first visit. It will be best if you see her when she's had a chance to get better."

"Oh." Sierra deftly used her chopsticks to snag a mushroom from one of the boxes. "Does she still have Ted?"

"Yes, she was holding it when I went in today."

"So it's helping her?"

"I think so. It certainly isn't hurting her."

Gail and Sierra made short work of the meal, their bites of spicy chicken and vegetables interspersed with short comments about their day.

They worked hard to maintain the tradition of eating together once a day. Gail knew finding the time was plenty hard with both their schedules and her almost teenaged daughter's mood swings, but she was glad they made the effort.

Gail finished the last piece of bok choy and wiped her mouth. "That was good. Sorry I wasn't home in time to make a meal."

"That's okay. I don't know why I was so worried when you weren't here."

"It is completely natural that we both will act a little more clingy considering what you just went through. If you forgive me, I'll forgive you."

"No prob."

"Want your fortune cookie?"

"Sure." Sierra cracked hers open and read, "'True friends joy in your success.'" She munched on the cookie. "What does yours say?"

"'Keep your eyes open. You never know what you might see.'"

"That one is better than mine. Can we trade?"

"No. Fortunes go to the ones who open them." Gail smiled and gathered the empty boxes. "I'll clean this up while you go and finish your homework."

"Okay." Sierra made it halfway up the stairs before she turned and came back down. "By the way, I don't have any clean uniforms for tomorrow."

"What?" Gail yelled. "Why didn't you put a load in when you got home?"

"It is part of my new philosophy."

"Philosophy?"

"Yeah, my philosophy of life."

"Let me get this right. You're eleven years old and you've got a philosophy of life." Gail shook her head. "I'm probably going to regret asking you this, but what is it?"

"I'm going to live each day as if it was my last."

"Okay," replied Gail. "What does that have to do with you not doing your chores?"

"Well, if this was the last day of your life, would *you* spend it doing laundry?"

Gail laughed involuntarily. She was still trying to find a way to refute that particular logic as she stayed up late washing, drying and ironing Sierra's clothes for the rest of the week, school uniforms, and Sierra's home and away soccer uniforms.

She should have been more upset at the accumulation of dirty clothes, but her own contribution to the pile took up most of one basket. Looking at the heap, she realized she had been getting low on more than just underwear.

Hours after she had originally planned, Gail finally climbed into bed. Her dreams were very disturbing, and she tossed and turned constantly. She was so exhausted the next morning that she almost slept through her alarm.

Taking one look at Gail's face when she entered the kitchen, Sierra quickly moved to pour her a cup of coffee. "Here. I'm guessing you don't want cream or sugar."

"You're right. I don't want it diluted." Gail put her face over the steaming mug. "When do you think you'll be home tonight?"

"I've got practice."

"You have a ride home?"

"Yeah. Janet's mom will bring me back."

"Okay. I'll probably be at the hospital again, but I should be here when you get home. I'm going to leave my phone on vibrate so call me if you need anything." Gail savored a mouthful of coffee. "What do you want for dinner?"

"Pizza?"

"All right. I'll order when I leave the hospital, and I'll put money on the counter in case it gets here before I do."

"Okay." Sierra slung her backpack over her shoulder and put her MUNI pass in her pocket. "Bye. If Lily wakes up, let her know I'm thinking of her."

"Of course, baby. Have a good day at school."

After Sierra left, Gail closed her eyes, the better to enjoy the house's silence and the remainder of her coffee. No matter how much of a liking she had taken to tea, she still could not start her day without some black gold.

Once she deemed herself sufficiently caffeinated, she headed into work. On arrival, she called Chet to join her in her office. He came in with his pad and pen ready.

"What's up, boss?" Chet asked.

"I want to be able to do as much work as possible on my laptop today."

"Why?"

"I'm going to spend as much of my days as I can at the hospital with Lily. I don't want to shirk my responsibilities, but I really need to be there with her."

"No problem. Let me sync your e-mail and you'll have all your inbox and calendar stuff at your fingertips."

"What about my documents?"

"I'll put your personal folder on a flash drive. There is a document in there telling you how to access the company cloud if you need manuals and stuff."

"We have a cloud?"

Chet rolled his eyes. "You know we do. You authorized moving the HR documents onto it three months ago as part of the disaster preparedness plan."

"You know I just sign what you put in front of me!" Taking the small flash drive from him, Gail asked, "Is this all I need?"

"You'll have to take your paperwork, but you'll be able to access most everything else from wherever you are."

Gail laughed in disbelief. "Okay, so if you could do all this, why am I still working from the office and not from my comfy chair at home?"

"Because that's not your management style."

She laughed. "Well, you're right. I do like to be hands-on, walking the walk."

"You go on," Chet waved her out of the office. "Oh, and give Lily my best wishes for a speedy recovery."

"I will."

A smile stayed on Gail's face while she made the drive to the hospital. Sitting down next to Wan in the waiting room, she pulled up an extra chair for her stuff, grinning at the look he gave her. "Well," she said. "You aren't actually paying me to sit here all day."

"I am extending you a certain latitude. I mean, I'm here, too."

"Yeah, but the boss can get away with more than us peons."

"I'd hardly call you a peon, Ms. Joiner." Wan laughed. "You know, I think that's the first time I've laughed since all this happened."

"I think we both needed it. How is Lily doing?"

"I'm sure they'll get her off the vent today. Once she's breathing on her own, they might even move her to a real room."

"That's great news." Gail pointed at the book in his hands. "What's that?"

Wan blushed. "Oh, she mentioned once that it was one of her favorite books."

"What's the title?"

"*The Wind in the Willows*. I've been reading a little every time I'm let in."

"That's a great idea." Gail squeezed his arm. "I'm sure she likes hearing you read a lot better than my babbling."

"I don't know. The nurses are still talking about how you got her to open her eyes."

"Her eyes opened, but I don't think she saw anything."

"It's a good sign, though." Looking at the doorway, Wan smiled at the waiting nurse. "Are you ready to take a turn?" he asked Gail.

"Thanks." Gail left her stuff piled up in the chair and walked across the room to join the nurse. "Good morning. How is she?"

"She's been a bit restless today."

"Isn't being restless a good thing?"

"We don't want her moving so much that she impedes the healing of her wounds. We like that she is still attempting to breathe on her own."

Sitting down in the room beside the bed, she was glad to find Lily still holding the teddy bear. "Hey, Lily. I'm back," she said. "I'll be here on and off for the next few hours. Unless you want me to continue to bore you silly, you need to wake up. Okay? Please wake up."

Lily stayed quiet and still. If not for the steady tone coming from the machine that followed every breath, Gail would not have known the injured woman was fighting to breathe. She continued to talk to Lily until her time was up.

Returning to the waiting room, Gail saw that Wan was engrossed in his book, so she quietly pulled a chair near to prop up her legs. Once she got comfortable, she set up the WiFi connection. She could remember when the only thing one could do in the hospital was read old magazines and watch soap operas. With the Internet connection, she could read her work e-mail and get the latest news stories about the accident.

Gail began looking through her inbox, finding a lot of e-mails had been sent following the press conference, and quite a few from other employees asking about Sierra and Lily. She concentrated on answering the e-mail from staff first.

Finishing up with work, she searched for any new news on the accident. From a story posted that morning, she learned the captain of the vessel that had plowed into their dock had died of a stroke at the wheel. The other officers on board had been distracted by his sudden collapse, but even putting the engines into full reverse had not slowed down the runaway container ship.

"Wow, did you know that when a ship is going full ahead, it can go three miles before the ship stops going forward?" she asked.

Wan looked up. "Three miles?"

"Yeah, it's called a crash stop, and depending on size and weight, the maneuver can take up to fifteen minutes." She turned her laptop. "Have you seen this update?" she asked Wan.

"Not sure. What does it say?"

"The captain died."

"Yeah. Our lawyers called to tell me."

"Lawyers?"

"Indeed. We've got to find a way to fix the damaged pier and replace the destroyed building as well as the stock. There are insurance company lawyers and our company's attorney who are getting together to make sure that we get all the compensation we can from the shipping company that owns the vessel."

"What about Lily's treatment?"

"Worker's compensation will pay for most of her treatment, and the shipping company's insurance should pay for anything extra or not covered."

"I've got the paperwork at the office. Do you want to take care of getting it filled out?"

"Yeah. I'll do it. I wouldn't want things to fall through the cracks."

"Now that would be embarrassing." Gail glanced up at the nurse. "It looks like it is your turn to visit."

"Oh, good."

After Wan's next visit, Dr. Thea Patterson came by on her rounds. The doctor and Wan hugged briefly before Wan reintroduced Gail to Lily's physician.

"We met last night," Gail said.

"Yes, your friend here got Lily to open her eyes," Dr. Patterson said.

"I knew it was a good idea for you to sit with her," Wan said to Gail. Turning to the doctor, he asked, "How's she doing?"

"Well, she's on her own now. We've taken her off the vent and will be monitoring her pretty closely for the rest of the day to make sure she continues to improve."

"And after that?" Wan asked.

At the same time, Gail asked, "Will she wake up soon?"

"We're hoping she will. I'll have another CAT scan run this afternoon to see if the swelling has abated in her skull. If it's clear and she's still unconscious, she may be in a coma, and we'll keep her here for at least another twenty-four hours for observation."

"When will she be moved to a private room so she can have more visitors?" Wan tapped his cell phone against his knee. "I've got a lot of people who want to come and see that she's really alive and offer her support."

"I'd like to get her out of the intensive care area as much as you do. But we don't want to rush to put her in a room with only occasional checks if there is the slightest chance she could have a relapse." Dr. Patterson slid her pen back into her pocket.

"So we really need her to wake up now?" Gail asked.

"That would be best."

"Thanks for stopping by, Dr. Patterson," Wan said. "We appreciate you giving us the update."

"It's not a problem. I just wish I had even better news to give you." Dr. Patterson smiled at them and walked out of the waiting room.

Wan left soon afterward to check in at work. Gail continued to visit throughout the afternoon. Lily started to mumble and shift more regularly.

When Gail was next in Lily's room, reading from the book Wan had left behind, the nurse noticed that Lily's blood pressure and pulse normalized. As an experiment, she allowed Gail to stay beyond the usual ten minutes.

For a long while, it seemed to work. Lily remained calm and still. After a couple of hours of Gail reading aloud, though, Lily began to shift under the sheet. The nurse encouraged her to touch and talk to Lily.

"Are you sure?" Gail looked from the nurse to Lily. "I don't want to hurt her."

"It will be good for her. Go ahead and try."

Gail gently reached out and walked her fingers across Lily's forehead. The brow under her fingertips furrowed. Lily's fingers twitched.

"That's good. She's reacting to you," the nurse said.

"Hey, Lily. Please wake up." Gail placed her palm on Lily's cheek and smiled when Lily seemed to nuzzle closer. "You are just too cute for words, and if I didn't think you'd kill me, I would tease you about it."

She felt a puff of air against the inside of her wrist. She glanced down to see Lily's lips move. "Doris, she's trying to say something."

"That's not all."

"What?"

"Look. Her eyes are open."

Gail quickly turned her head, grinning when Lily looked at her. "Welcome back, Lily."

Lily looked at Gail with no sense of recognition, just confusion. When the nurse moved, her eyes tracked, but whatever she saw seemed to disturb her. She managed to get her uninjured arm under her and tried to push up.

Doris frowned at the telemetry readings. "Try and keep her from moving too much. I'll be right back."

"Okay," Gail said, pressing Lily back onto the bed. "You've got to stay calm, sweetie."

Lily continued to struggle and kept trying to move.

"I can't hold her still," Gail called, worried about the blood soaking through the back of Lily's gown.

"Here. Let me give her this." Doris injected a sedative into Lily's IV.

As Lily relaxed and her eyes closed, Gail played with the damp tendrils of hair on the back of Lily's neck. "Just sleep. You'll remember more the next time you wake up."

Once Lily was sound asleep, Gail stood up and backed away from the bed. "You saw that, didn't you?"

The nurse busied herself with cleaning fresh blood off her patient.

Gail started to pace. "She didn't know who I was. Does she have amnesia?"

"It is common when someone has had a brain trauma for them to be disoriented when they first wake up."

"So this might not be permanent?"

"Not necessarily. True amnesia is pretty rare. Give her a little more time. Bad things happened. Her body shut down for a bit to recover. You can't expect her to just bounce back from that."

"No. I guess not." Gail picked up the teddy bear that had been knocked to the floor during the struggle. She kissed it on the nose and tucked it under Lily's hand. "I guess I'll go now."

"She'll be out for at least six hours. You can come back during tomorrow's visiting hours." Doris smiled. "She might even be in her own room by then."

"I hope so."

Gail went back to the waiting room and sent an e-mail to the company that Lily had briefly regained consciousness. She thanked everyone for their thoughts and prayers, and then called Wan to tell him what she had just experienced and let him know she was heading home.

"Are you sure?" he asked.

"Yeah, with that last shot, she's going to be out until after I have to leave, so I'm going to go home now. I've got a lot of chores to do, and it will be nice to eat a home-cooked meal for a change."

"I understand. I'll let you know if anything happens tonight."

"Thanks, Wan. Good night."

Hanging up the phone, Gail finished packing her paperwork and her laptop. She carried everything out to her car and gratefully consigned it to the trunk. No way she was going to bring it all into her house, she thought as she drove home. She would take the laptop in to check her e-mail, but she meant what she'd said to Wan. Tonight was about family and neglected chores.

Gail pulled the car into her driveway. On her way inside the house, she picked up the newspaper she had forgotten to bring in when she'd left that morning. Once inside, she pulled a couple of chicken breasts out of the freezer and put them on the counter to defrost.

Dinner preparations underway, it was time to clean bathrooms, dust and vacuum. She cleaned like a woman possessed. She had the house shining like a new dime when Sierra came home from soccer practice.

Gail looked up from washing the last dish and grinned at the surprised look on her daughter's face. "Hey, kiddo. How was school and practice?"

"Um, fine." Sierra breathed in deeply. Gail knew she smelled orange cleaner, bleach and a whiff of ammonia. "Who are you and what have you done with my mother?"

"What, can't a woman decide to be a homemaker for once?"

Sierra glanced around. "I'm not complaining. Heck, you could have waited to make me do it." She shrugged. "Whatever makes you happy. I'm going to take a shower. When does the pizza get here?"

"Oh, I'm making lemon chicken instead. It's a new recipe I found in the *Louisiana Cookin'* magazine your grandmother sent me."

"You're cooking, too? What's up?"

"What?"

"You only cook new things when you've had a good day."

"Lily woke up again today." When Sierra yelled jubilantly, she held up her hands. "She's not out of the woods yet. She'll have a long recovery to face."

"When can I see her?"

"Once she gets moved."

"When will that be?"

"I'm hoping tomorrow."

Sierra pouted. "I've got a game in the afternoon."

"I know. It will probably be Saturday before I'm able to get you over there." Gail ruffled her daughter's hair. "Anyway, it will probably be better for you to give her another day or two to get better. You can be quite the handful."

"All right," replied Sierra. "But I really want to see her."

"You will." Gail kissed Sierra's forehead, and then made a face when she licked her lips. "Eww. Salty. Go shower."

"Yes, Mom."

Gail and Sierra enjoyed a lovely dinner and an early night.

The next morning, Gail was pleased to find a voice mail from Wan telling her that Lily had woken up again and been moved to a private room.

She called her office to let Chet know she would be at the hospital another day. He seemed pleased to reroute her work to her laptop again, especially after hearing about Lily's continued recovery.

On her arrival at the hospital, Gail went to the intensive care unit where she was told Lily had been moved. The nurse told her how to find the right wing, but she got lost twice, finding it a little confusing to locate the correct room among all the others that looked the same. Finally, she opened the right door.

She recognized the bandages swathing Lily's head. Her arm was still in a cast. Lily lay on her side, panting slightly. It was almost reassuring that she was no longer hooked to so many machines.

Quietly, Gail sat down next to the bed, set up her laptop and papers, and began to work. She occasionally talked about an employee issue just so Lily could hear her voice.

When Lily woke, her gaze went straight to Gail. "Ga…" she croaked.

Gail looked up from her laptop and smiled. "Hey, I didn't expect you to wake up for a while."

"Wha…" Lily started to say before she was interrupted by a cough.

"Here, have some water." Gail grabbed a cup of water off the table. Extending the straw, she placed it against Lily's lips. The woman stared at her for a moment before drawing the water greedily down. "Slow down," she warned. "Don't drink too much too fast."

Lily released the straw and laid her head back down, panting from the exertion. She closed her eyes.

"Do you want any more?" Gail asked.

"No…not now." Lily licked her lips and asked, "Why you here?"

"I came to check on you."

"Huh?" Lily thought for a moment. "Sierra okay?" She sounded worried, and tried to push herself up from the bed.

"Whoa, don't move." Gail pressed her back down. "Sierra's fine, thanks to you. She's worried about you."

"Oh." Lily blinked owlishly. "You want statement?"

"Statement?"

"For insurance."

"No, Lily. I'm just here to see you. To be with you."

"Don't understand. We don't do that."

"I think that needs to change." Gail considered the sweat beading Lily's forehead. "Are you in pain?"

"Yeah. Hurts."

Gail reached down to pick up the administration button for the intravenous pain reliever. "Press this and it will take the pain away," she said, trying to get Lily to take it.

"No." Lily moved her hand away. "Don't want to sleep."

"Lily, please. Listen to your body. You've suffered a severe trauma."

Lily continued to refuse. Suddenly she stiffened.

"What's wrong?"

"Back...my back."

Gail frantically pushed the call button. Finally, a nurse came in. She took one look at Lily and tapped a code on the pain drip. An extra dose of medication quickly slid in her IV and down into her veins.

Muscle by muscle, Lily slowly relaxed.

After she fell asleep, the nurse tried to get Gail to leave. "I need to see if she pulled any stitches. It is not a pretty sight."

"I've already seen the damage when she was upstairs in intensive care."

Shrugging, the nurse peeled back the bandages on Lily's back.

Gail's heart clenched when she saw the wounds again. There was still a lot of swelling in Lily's lower back. She saw signs of tension in the muscles. Without a second thought, she reached out and gently massaged the back of Lily's neck.

Slowly, almost imperceptibly, Lily went boneless. The combination of pain relief and the soothing touch proved enough to put her completely out.

The nurse took Lily's vitals and finally nodded. "All right. She'll be out for a while. That was a big dose I just gave her."

Gail smiled. "Thank you for your help."

"It's my job."

"Well, you did a good one here. Thank you."

The nurse blushed and held out her hand. "I'm Tamika. I work the day shift."

"I'm Gail."

"Nice to meet you. What happened to her?"

"You heard about that ship crashing into the dock the other day and destroying a warehouse?" Gail waited for Tamika's nod. "Well, she was one of the people in the building. My daughter was the other, and she walked out without hardly a scratch thanks to Lily." She stroked Lily's dark hair. "I was so scared."

"It is normal for patients to struggle a bit when they first regain consciousness," Tamika said. "This isn't a bad thing."

"I know. It's just hard to reconcile the active person I know with the woman stuck in this bed."

"Even if she doesn't regain the use of her legs, she'll be the same person. Come on, just think of how much easier it will be catch her."

Gail blushed hotly.

With a smirk, Tamika left to tend to other patients.

For a while, Gail watched Lily sleeping. Do I want to catch her? she wondered. Just a few days ago, we disliked each other. Could I trust these new feelings? she asked herself. More importantly, would Lily want to be caught?

CHAPTER NINE

The next day, Gail got on the phone with Lily's doctor and the nurses working on her floor. She used their information on hospital routines to come up with a schedule for Lily's friends and co-workers who wanted to visit.

She tried to make sure that none of the visits would be too long, and tried not to schedule anyone past visiting hours. She did not want the staff at the hospital to become their enemies because of a careless disregard for the rules. She knew that once Lily started physical therapy, things were going to change, but for now, the schedule she'd drafted appeared to be workable.

Almost too well, she thought a little later. She had posted the schedule on the company's intranet and the slots filled up very quickly. It was almost three o'clock before she could drive over to the hospital to take the first free block on the schedule.

The number of people who had signed up amazed her. Only later, when she remembered she had not put her name on the list, did she realize what she had done. Having to share Lily with so many other people was hard to get used to. She actually felt a little jealous that her co-workers were so seriously impacting her visits with Lily.

The first thing she noticed when she entered the room was that Lily looked drained. She had dark circles under her eyes and she was sweating.

"Are you in pain?" Gail asked.

Lily's eyes snapped open. "Would you like me to be?" she asked.

"Of course not. Why do you ask that?"

"I don't know. My head hurts."

Gail pulled a chair over and sat down beside the bed at eye level with Lily so she wouldn't have to strain to look at her. Resting her fingers on the back of Lily's hand, she said, "I've been thinking ever since this happened about why we fight so much."

"You look down on me."

"Oh, Lily."

"It's true."

"No, it isn't. I never looked down on you. I was jealous of you." Gail blew out a breath. "You had it all and it was all so effortless."

"What do you mean?"

"Everybody loves you and you do your job so well." Gail waved her hands. "This is the first time that I could see you today because so many people wanted to visit. I sure don't have that sort of effect on my co-workers."

"You're still new."

Gail shook her head. "Not even at my other job could I count on so many co-workers to care for me, and I was there almost five years." She sighed. "And it annoyed me that there are never any complaints from your department."

"You want complaints?"

"I'm in human resources. We live from crisis to crisis, and if there aren't any, we hardly know what to do with ourselves."

"That's not true. You do really well to calm things down and head off trouble. Lots of those new policies and procedures made sense."

Gail grinned. "But not all?"

Blushing, Lily sputtered. "I already have a lot to do without all those extra memos and reports to complete."

"It's okay. I know these procedures add work to the already overburdened managers. They will make your lives easier in the long run, though."

"I know that. I just felt like I had to put up a fight." Lily dropped her gaze. "You seemed to be everywhere. Taking over." She continued through gritted teeth, "I have never known how to deal with beautiful women."

Gail smiled until her cheeks hurt. She could not help the thrill she felt in knowing that Lily thought she was beautiful.

"All the guys seem to fall at your feet to do your bidding, and I guess...I guess I was jealous, too."

"We don't have to be jealous of each other. We could be friends."

"As soon as we go back to work, we're going to put all this behind us, and it will be business as usual."

"No." Gail spoke emphatically.

"What?"

"I said no. I'm not going back to the way we were."

"Why not?" Lily slammed her hand down on the bed. "Don't be treating me differently just because I'm crippled."

"Okay, I hardly know where to begin with that statement. In the first place, I can't go back to the way it was because I don't want to be that person anymore." Gail stood up and began to pace. "When I reflect on how much energy I put into examining each and every interaction we had to find the slight I was sure was there, I'm furious with myself. I think we both have better uses for our time and energy."

Lily grunted.

"I also know more about you than I did before," Gail went on, "and I've got too much respect for you to treat you the same way."

"What did Wan say?"

"What?"

"Wan. He obviously got to you."

"Got to me? No. He and I spoke." Gail sank back into the chair. "Just like Chet and I spoke. I've learned some pretty amazing things. Wan told me about how you two met and a little about your past."

"He had no right."

"Lily, he didn't break any confidences. What he told me made me admire you even more."

"I don't understand what you mean."

"The woman I thought you were would never have done what you did."

"Huh?"

"You saved my daughter." Gail ticked off on her fingers. "At great personal risk, you pushed her to a safe place. You know she only had a few scratches, right?" Waiting for a nod, she smiled. "You treated her with dignity and respect while you were both under the rubble. Then you risked your life again when you insisted the rescuers get her out first."

"I didn't do anything special."

"I beg to differ. You are the bravest person I have ever known."

"I did what I had to."

"Yes. That's my point. You're the sort of person who finds such acts natural. You are not the petty, spiteful woman that I assumed you were."

"Oh."

"Even Chet has been on my case about my assumptions about you. I'm happy to say I'm finally listening to him."

"Really?"

"Yeah. I was wrong and I'm sorry about my part in making things between us worse." Gail leaned closer. "Even if you have lingering physical challenges from this, you will never be impaired in my eyes."

Lily's eyes glistened with tears. "I want to be able to walk, but I wouldn't trade the use of my legs for Sierra's life."

"I know that."

Suddenly, Lily yawned widely. "I'm tired."

"I'm not surprised. You've had a busy day."

"Lots of people," Lily mumbled.

"Yeah. There are a lot of people who care about you. They needed to see for themselves that you were okay." Gail spoke softly, smiling when Lily dropped off to sleep. With the head injury and the emotional discussion, it was a wonder she had not passed out sooner.

Once she was sure Lily was asleep, Gail left the room and stopped, surprised to see Wan pacing in the hallway. "Hello. Why didn't you come in?"

"The two of you were talking and I didn't want to interrupt." Wan looked down the hallway as he spoke.

"How much did you hear?"

"Most of it." He looked at her. "You're very brave to go walking through the minefield that is Lily's psyche."

"It needed to be said. I hope I didn't make things tough for you. She seemed a little angry that you and I had talked."

"She'll get over it. That's what friends do, right? They forgive each other."

"Yeah. I...uh...I like her. I'd like for us to be friends."

Wan winked. "Friends. Gotcha."

For perhaps the millionth time in her life, Gail cursed her light complexion and the ease with which she blushed.

"That brings me to a nice segue," Wan said.

"Oh?"

"Yes. I have a favor to ask."

"Go on."

"It's just that you've got a house and a yard and all, right?"

"Yes, my place in Glen Park has a small fenced yard."

"I don't."

Gail did not see where the conversation was leading. "You want to throw a party to celebrate her waking up?"

"No. That's a good idea, but no. See, I've been taking care of Lily's dog since the accident. I live in a condo and my place is totally not set up for a big dog." He made a moue of distaste. "There is slobber and fur on all my lovely things!"

"What's her name?"

"Butch."

"Butch? Why in the world?"

He laughed. "Because she looks so tough, but if you treat her right, she'll roll on her back and show you her belly. A good tummy rub will make you a goddess in her eyes."

"How big a dog?"

"She's a Lab mix."

"Mixed with what?"

"Who knows? It could be anything. I don't know anything about dogs. She could a little bit of everything but, honestly, she's just a sweetheart of a mutt that Lily rescued."

"Rescued from what?"

"There are still kill shelters around. She was going to be put down because she was too old. Most people want puppies, not adult dogs. Lily saved her life," Wan said with a smile.

"She seems to make a habit of rescuing people in distress."

"That's our Lily. Really, though, I think Butch would be happier with you and Sierra." Wan paused, and then added, "I know I'll be happier knowing you took her in."

Gail shook her head. "Sierra has been bugging me for a dog for years, but I've always been too worried about our crazy schedules and the extra work to cave."

"That is perfect, then. You get to take a dog on a trial basis to see if you two can handle it and I get the dog hair out of my house."

"What if Sierra falls in love with the dog? How is it going to be when the dog has to go back home with Lily?"

"That will give you and Lily plenty of time to be friends together while Sierra gets to play with the dog." Wan grinned. "Well, will you?"

"Tell me a little more about what's involved."

"She's a great dog. Very sweet with kids and women, but a little skittish around men."

Gail raised her eyebrow.

Lowering his voice to a near whisper, Wan said, "I don't think the dog knows what to make of me. I mean, I may act one way at work, but at home I let my hair down." He batted his eyelashes.

Gail laughed until a disapproving glare from a passing nurse sobered her up.

Wan shrugged. "All I know is that Lily got the dog after her last breakup. I think she did it to remind herself not to make the same mistakes."

"What sort of mistakes?"

"Believing everything a pretty girl says." Wan looked her in the eyes. "I probably shouldn't be telling you any of this."

"Any of what?"

"I have the feeling that you and Lily could really have something together. I don't want to say something to screw things up, but I also don't want to give you so much information that you run away."

Gail ducked her head and stared at the floor. "Things seem to be happening so fast. I almost don't trust my feelings here."

"What are you feeling?"

"It's like I've spun a hundred and eighty degrees. We weren't friends at all and I didn't like her before all this happened."

"There's a thin line between love and hate," Wan sang.

Gail slapped his arm. "Be serious. Is the stress of nearly losing Sierra affecting my judgment? What is real?"

"I always thought it was a shame that the two of you didn't hit it off when you first met."

"We're lucky we didn't hit each other," Gail mumbled.

"I don't think it was that bad, was it?"

"She just aggravated and questioned me at every turn."

"And you were innocent?"

Blushing, Gail confessed, "No, I would sometimes do things I knew would provoke her, just to see her reaction."

"Like that memo on office toys?"

"I can't believe she thinks Nerf guns are an appropriate management tool. Someone could get hurt horseplaying in the warehouse and the company would be liable for it."

"I've always given her leeway because she gets results. The entire distribution network runs smoothly because of her. Besides, those games were usually pretty tame and provided much needed stress relief." Wan winked. "I was always envious that I couldn't use them during board meetings."

"Even so," Gail rubbed her temples. "Mentally and emotionally changing direction like this has me going insane."

"I don't think it's crazy for the two of you to finally get past whatever was blocking you. Cataclysmic events often lead to a realigning of priorities. While it may seem fast, that doesn't mean it isn't real or right."

"I hope so. I would like to get to know her better."

"I think I should tell you more about her ex, then."

"You can tell me. I will keep your confidence."

"Lily got taken to the cleaners by her last girlfriend. Her ex ran up a huge credit card debt in her name, emptied all of her bank accounts, and stole most of the stuff out of her house while she was at work."

"What a bitch!" Gail clenched her fists, angry that anyone could be so cruel. "Did Lily press charges?"

"No, she was too shattered and embarrassed to make a public scene."

"That's just horrible."

"You got that right. Thought she'd found true love and it turned out she was just being played."

"She hasn't seen anyone since?"

"No one serious. There were a few girls on her team and in her soccer league who wanted some playing time off the field, but she shut herself off."

"What team?"

He looked surprised. "Oh, I thought you knew. She plays soccer. Pretty seriously, too."

"I didn't know that."

"Yeah. I think that will be the hardest thing to give up if she can't get her mobility back. She's signed up to play in the next Gay Games in Ohio."

"Really?"

"Yeah. Her team has traveled to Sydney, Chicago and Cologne. They've got their eyes on the prize for the next go-round."

Lost in her thoughts for a moment, Gail pictured Lily wearing shorts and running down a soccer field. She shook herself out of the daydream when she realized Wan had started giving her directions to his condominium.

"Why don't I just follow you?" she asked.

"Good idea. You know what I drive?"

"Hmm, I don't know. Could you be the one who drives the silver Beamer that is always parked in the president's space?"

"Yeah, that's the one." Wan grinned. "What do you drive?"

"A green CR-V. I'm in the parking garage on Baker."

"Me, too."

The journey to his North Beach condo was fairly uneventful. Wan only ran one yellow light before he slowed down and made it easy for her to keep up.

Gail was worried about the dog. She knew Sierra would be ecstatic to help Lily out this way, but she was concerned about taking on the responsibility for an animal. She worked full time and Sierra had a lot of after-school activities.

As she parked her car, she just hoped they could do a good enough job.

Wan unlocked the door and slowly opened it. Gail heard the sound of a dog charging toward them. "Don't worry. Butch'll be happy to see you," he said.

He pushed the door wide open. She watched as the dog went from a full run to a skidding stop in the space of a foot. The black and tan animal sat down, warily wagging her tail.

"Now, don't take it personally," Wan said.

"What?"

"Watch."

Wan held out his hand and the dog dutifully sniffed. The big head turned to Gail and sniffed the air around her. Butch's ears straightened and a plaintive whine came out of her muzzle. The big tail swept quickly back and forth.

"Um, what is this?" asked Gail. She began to scratch behind Butch's ears.

"I don't know." Wan watched as the dog seemed to melt under her touch. "I have no idea. Butch is usually pretty standoffish when she first meets someone. She only gradually seems to accept them."

"Maybe it's because I smell like Lily. I did touch her while I was talking to her."

"That's probably it." Wan shrugged and walked into the main room. "Just make yourself comfortable. I'm going to go and collect her stuff."

"How much stuff are we talking about?"

"What do you care? You've got a honking huge car!"

"Yeah, but I'll have to carry it into the house."

"Make Sierra do it. I mean, isn't that why people have kids? So they have someone to do the chores?"

"Seriously? Is that why your parents had you?" Gail wagged her finger at him. "I didn't get pregnant to have a servant and I would have been a fool if I had. Kids make a helluva lot more mess than they ever clean up! That being said, I'm sure Sierra will be excited to do it for Lily and for the chance to finally get a dog."

"Sounds like she's developing a crush."

"I don't know. I think some of it's because Lily treated her like an adult while they were trapped together. My kid is wicked smart and she hates being condescended to, which is how most adults treat kids."

"I used to hate that, too."

"We all did. That's why it's so strange that when we're adults, we do the same things to kids that we disliked when we were children."

"Can I ask you a question?"

"Sure," replied Gail. "I reserve the right to refuse to answer, though."

"How did you get Sierra? I mean, with that hair, she's obviously got your genes, so I'm assuming you gave birth to her."

"She definitely came out of me. Shall I tell you how many hours I was in labor?"

"No thanks. I just mean...um...was it a turkey baster or something?"

"Oh, you mean the whole 'how does a lesbian conceive a child' thing?"

"Yeah."

"I wasn't always a lesbian." Gail paused. "Strike that. I wasn't always willing to be a lesbian."

"What do you mean?"

"I was married to Sierra's father."

Wan's eyes popped open. "Really?"

"Yeah. It was what my family wanted. I knew I liked women, but I hardly had extensive experience and I never had a serious relationship. I certainly wasn't out to my parents. Jared was a family friend and always seemed to be around, ready to go to the movies or catch a meal. My parents thought he was great and it just seemed easiest to go along with it."

"Go along?"

"Looking back, it seems like everyone else was making the plans. Until he proposed, I would have said he wasn't my boyfriend, but a boy who was a friend. As he had been old fashioned enough to go to my parents for permission, everyone figured it was a done deal.

"My mom was a whirlwind when it came to orchestrating the wedding. The path of least resistance led me through the engagement and had me up at the altar before I really knew what hit me." She laughed. "I never really got the hang of having to use protection, and before I knew it, I was pregnant."

"You wanted Sierra?"

"I wanted her more than I wanted the marriage. I knew we were in trouble the day after the wedding when I woke up with him in the same bed." Gail laughed. "Men are gross in the morning. Everything from waking erections to stubbled cheeks, all the grunts and noises. I hated it."

Wan laughed with her. "I can't argue with you about that." He paused. "Do you mind me asking about this stuff?"

"Not really. I think this whole situation has both of us sharing more than we might have within the usual boundaries of the boss-and-employee relationship."

"I hope I was more that just your boss before all this." Wan smirked. "We've broken many of the barriers between us already in our talks at the hospital."

"Yeah, getting to know you better has been a definite bonus of this whole situation."

"And changing your mind about Lily."

Gail nodded. "You're right. I can't think of her the same any more."

"That makes me even happier that I convinced you to take Butch." Wan leaned against the wall. "If you're comfortable telling me, what happened to your marriage?"

"I had Sierra, and Jared and I said goodbye."

"It can't have been that easy."

"No, there were things said and things thrown, but it came down to a reality check and the fact that we had nothing in common. We parted as not quite friends, but not enemies." Gail sighed. "I wish I could say that it was the great passion of my life, but even now, there are days I can hardly believe that I was that person, willing to marry a virtual stranger, and a man at that."

"Is he involved in your lives now?"

"He does a lot of international work with his company and he spends most of the year out of the country. Whenever he's in town, he tries to come by, but to her, he's not so much a dad as a guy bearing cool gifts."

"How did your mom take your breakup?"

"Remarkably well. Once she got a chance to hold her grandchild, she was pretty okay with the divorce and my coming out to her."

"It's great that you have a good relationship with her."

"She's always there to babysit. It was like there was a checklist in her mind of what was expected, and once an item got checked off, it didn't matter anymore. Good school, husband, child, all checked off."

"Has she been okay with your life since then?"

"I've only had a couple of serious relationships since then and you already know about one. Sierra has always been my priority and frankly, my excuse to not get too close to people."

"Lily is good with kids."

"Sierra is proof positive of that, but enough serious stuff. Let's talk doggies." Gail sat down on the couch and found herself eye to eye with Butch. She marveled at the soft fur and got lost in the liquid brown eyes. "She's beautiful."

"She's also a bed hog, so watch yourself."

"I can hardly believe you let a dog join you on what must be six million thread count sheets."

Wan blushed. "Well, Butch looks so pathetic that it broke my heart to make her sleep on the floor."

"It's a dog!"

"You say that now. I bet you change your tune tonight."

"Whatever." Gail made a W sign with her fingers and thumbs. "Is there anything else I need to know?"

"She is fed twice a day, I take her for two long walks morning and afternoon and Bobby takes her out around lunch and dinnertime." Wan ticked things off on his fingers. "There's no medication for her, but she needs regular brushing or you'll be overrun in loose hair. There is a tooth cleaning chew she is supposed to get twice a week."

"Sounds manageable. Why don't you get her stuff while I get to know her a little better?"

"Right. Just hang out there. I'll be back."

Gail lost herself in petting the big dog, so much so that she was startled when Wan appeared with an armload of supplies. The dog watched intently while Gail and Wan took her bed, bowl and food out the door. After loading everything in the car, they returned to the condo.

Handing Gail the leash, Wan said, "Here you go. Let me know if you have any problems at all. There are probably members of Lily's team who could take her, if it is an issue."

"Why didn't you ask them?"

"Because of my eavesdropping. Some might call it meddling, but I think you and Sierra keeping the dog is the best thing for all three of you."

"Thanks, I think."

"Don't mention it." Wan waved her off.

Gail started walking down the front steps. She stopped and cocked her head. Was that the sound of a vacuum cleaner coming from inside Wan's house? She shrugged and focused on getting Butch into the car.

After arriving home, she found it easy to get the dog settled. As soon as she released the leash, Butch explored the entire house from top to bottom at a near run. She returned after Gail set out a clean bowl of water, and sat down, looking sadly at her.

"I know," Gail said. "Your mom is not here. You've got to stay with us for a while, but as soon as she can, your mom will take you home."

The big dog huffed out a gust of air and lay down in front of the door. Gail smiled and went into her home office. She turned on her laptop and began to deal with the e-mails from work that had come in after she'd left for the day.

Engrossed in her work, she was startled by a squeal and a woof. Scared of what might be happening to her daughter, Gail rushed to the front door only to find Sierra rolling on the floor with the dog.

"Sierra," she called frantically.

Her daughter sat up with a huge smile on her face. "We got a dog?"

Breathing a sigh of relief, Gail replied, "It's actually Lily's dog."

Sierra threw her arms around Butch and dragged the hundred pound dog into her lap. "That's so cool."

"We have to take good care of her while Lily's in the hospital, but you have to remember she isn't our dog. We will have to give her back."

Butch wagged her tail, looking adoringly into Sierra's eyes, while Sierra stroked and petted her, clearly not listening to a word of Gail's admonition.

"I'm serious, Sierra. Don't fall in love."

"Too late," Sierra saucily replied.

"Fine. You'll need to make sure the dog always has clean water, is fed twice a day and gets lots of exercise. You'll also need to be on poop patrol when you take her out."

"What's her name? Can I take her to practice?"

"Her name is Butch."

"That's a funny name for a girl."

"Isn't it, though? We can ask Lily tomorrow if it is okay for Butch to go to soccer with you."

"Ask Lily?" Sierra jumped to her feet. "I get to see her?"

"Yes. We're going to go in the morning."

Sierra flung herself into Gail's arms. "Thank you. Thank you. This is turning into the best day ever."

"What else good happened?"

"I aced my math test and my speech in Spanish went really well."

"Great, honey. Why don't you come in and tell me all about it while I make dinner?"

Gail was so happy to see her daughter laughing and smiling that she could not bring herself to scold Sierra when she fed

Butch from the table. Sierra even offered to take Butch for a walk after dinner.

"You bet you will. You can consider this a trial run on dog ownership and I expect you to take responsibility for her getting exercise. We can't just let her out in the backyard. She will need to be walked after dinner and walked in the morning before school, too. Make sure you set your alarm for earlier."

"Okay," Sierra agreed eagerly.

Gail made sure Sierra had a plastic bag and waved them off on their walk. She wondered how long it would take for the joy of dog ownership to become a burden.

She had put the dog bed in her room, but it became immediately clear at bedtime that Butch would be sleeping with Sierra. No amount of arguing dissuaded her daughter.

"The dog is almost bigger than your bed," Gail pointed out.

"It's okay. We fit."

She sighed. "Make her get in her own bed when you find out that she doesn't."

Figuring Sierra's resultant promise meant next to nothing, Gail threw her hands up in the air and went to her own bedroom. She found it easy to fall asleep, although she did wake up in the middle of the night sweating and clinging to the edge of her bed.

When she rolled over, she saw that Butch had joined her in the bed and was sleeping lengthwise across the mattress. Too tired to do anything about it, she fell back asleep.

At breakfast, Sierra sulked and played with her food.

"What's wrong?" Gail asked.

"You."

"Excuse me?"

"You were telling me about how I wasn't supposed to let Butch sleep with me, and then you go and make her get into your bed."

"Okay, a little misconception here. I didn't make her get into bed with me. I woke up and she was there."

"You didn't kick her off, though."

"No. And, before you ask, I don't know why. I do know that I want you to adjust your attitude. I'm not inflicting your bad mood on Lily."

"I'm not mad at her."

"Well, you shouldn't be mad at me."

Sierra kicked her feet against the rungs of her chair. Finally, she said, "I'm sorry, Mom. I'm not really mad at you. I guess I'm a little jealous that Butch slept with you."

"That is quite all right. You're entitled to feel jealous, but your sulking is another thing entirely. Do you understand the difference?"

"Yes, ma'am. I'm sorry."

"Me, too. I could hardly sleep with that hot, furry blanket on the bed with me." Gail put her coffee cup in the dishwasher. "Now, are you ready to go visiting?"

"Yes." Sierra leapt out of her chair.

"Wait. We've got to make sure the dog is taken care of. Has she got food and water?"

"Check."

"Let her outside and see if she needs to go."

Sierra yelled for Butch and pounded downstairs to the basement entrance to the backyard before the last word cleared Gail's lips. She smiled as the large dog chased after her daughter obediently. Ah, she mused, if only her child stayed like this and did not act like a brat on a regular basis.

While she drove to the hospital, Gail tried to talk to Sierra about ground rules. Sierra kept playing with the radio and her window until Gail lost her temper.

"Stop it. Just sit still." Gail took a deep breath. "What I am telling you is very serious. You know Lily was hurt badly, but it will be a different thing to see her in the hospital bed. You need to make sure you speak quietly."

"I know not to yell."

"Good. You also need to not talk a hundred miles an hour. She's on drugs to manage the pain and they make her have a hard time focusing." Glancing at Sierra, she went on, "Lily may also be asleep or have other visitors. We'll have to be really patient."

Sierra giggled.

"What's so funny?"

"I was just thinking 'be patient with the patient.'"

"Yes. Good one." Gail pulled into the hospital's parking lot and found a space near the elevator bank. When they left the elevator on Lily's floor, she took Sierra's hand. "No running."

"Aw, Mom. I wasn't."

"I can see you're excited, but you need to calm down."

"What if she doesn't remember me?"

"Honey, you're almost the first thing she asked about after she woke up. She was worried about you."

"Really?"

"Yes. She couldn't see you and did not know if you were really okay when the firefighters took you out of the warehouse."

"Oh." Sierra's eyes grew big. "We were worried about each other," she said with wonder in her voice.

"Yep. That is why I think this visit is important for both of you. I believe you and Lily need to see that each other is alive and, if not well, getting better every day." Gail stopped at the door to Lily's room. "Wait here a minute."

"Why?"

"I want to make sure she is able to see you."

Sierra looked mulish. Gail knew she would have a fight on her hands if her daughter did not see her idol soon. "Remember what we talked about earlier about your attitude. Trust me, this will only take a moment," she said reassuringly.

Peeking in, she saw that Lily was alone. Gail walked around the bed, finding Lily's eyes were open. She was staring at the teddy bear in her hand.

"Good morning," Gail said.

"Oh, hey." Lily blinked at her. "You're here early."

"I brought someone to see you. Are you up for visitors?"

"Sure."

Gail went to the door, opened it, and waved Sierra through. She watched Sierra make her way to the other side of the bed. From where she stood, she saw her daughter's face light up when she saw Lily for the first time since the accident.

Smiling, Gail leaned against the door and watched as two of her favorite people chattered like magpies for almost a solid hour. She learned a lot about her daughter's soccer team from Lily's knowledgeable questions.

Eventually, the nurse came in to take Lily's vitals. When she manipulated Lily's back, the injured woman tried to fight back a groan. She was in obvious pain.

Sierra stepped to the bedside and gently stroked Lily's hair. Gail thought the caretaking was a side of her daughter she had not seen before.

"Aren't you going to do anything?" Sierra demanded.

"Excuse me?" asked the nurse.

"Can't you tell that she's hurting?"

"Well, I could give her muscle relaxant, but then she'll likely sleep for the rest of visiting hours." The nurse studied Sierra, who was fiercely holding Lily's hand. "Does she want a shot?"

Lily tried to shake her head. Her back muscles spasmed again. "Don't want to sleep," she mumbled.

"Well, I don't want you to hurt," Sierra told her. "It scares me to see you in pain."

Breathing carefully, Lily opened her eyes. "I don't want you to be scared anymore."

"Then take the shot."

Unable to argue, Lily gritted her teeth and asked for the drug.

The nurse quickly returned with a syringe for an injection directly into Lily's back, and then came over to the door where Gail was standing and winked at her. "That is quite a kid you've got there. Ms. Rush never wants to take the entire dosage of pain medication."

"She can be a handful," Gail answered, thinking about their many workplace tussles.

"Well, the patient's just putty in that girl's hands."

Gail laughed. "Thanks. I'm Gail and that's my daughter, Sierra."

"Pleased to meet you. I'm Wyn. I work mainly overnights on weekends, so you'll only see me in the mornings."

"Good to know. We'll be back tomorrow."

"If your daughter manages to keep Lily complacent like that, we may have to hire her," the nurse said as she left.

Gail and Sierra took their leave after Sierra finished singing a lullaby and making sure the teddy bear was firmly nestled in Lily's hand.

Gail beamed in pride while walking Sierra back to the car. Her daughter was growing very fast and developing into a beautiful woman inside and out.

CHAPTER TEN

Two nights later, Gail made another circuit of her house, wandering from room to room until she completed another lap. Part of her mind idly wondered how many miles she might have paced, but most of her thoughts were consumed with Sierra.

It was the first night since the accident that Sierra spent away from home. Gail groused to herself that if the trip to Santa Monica for a soccer tournament had not been scheduled months in advance, she would have found a way to keep her daughter home.

She stopped pacing occasionally to straighten up. It seemed to her that when Sierra had gotten ready for her excursion, she had felt compelled to wreck the house in the process. Small piles of snacks covered the counters and table, and the clothes from her dresser had migrated around the house as though a small tornado had ripped through the place.

Gail compared the frantic packing, screaming and running around from last night to this too-quiet home. Despite her lack of patience with Sierra yesterday, she dearly missed the comfort and chaos her noisy, moody daughter brought to her life.

For a while, Butch had followed her from room to room. The dog's patience was finite, though, and now Butch slept on the couch with her head between her paws, her dark gaze worriedly following Gail's progress whenever she was in view.

When she walked by, Gail petted Butch and gave her a comforting smile. The dog was no more fooled by the attempt to comfort than she was.

Gail sighed and started another circuit.

She did not know what to do with herself. There was nothing on television, and she had surfed through several hundred digital channels enough times to make absolutely sure. She had read the day's paper with her coffee in the morning and put it in the recycling bin, which had been picked up today so she did not even have the classifieds to read.

Running her fingers along a bookshelf, she found nothing tempting, but realized that everything needed a good dusting. She satisfied herself with blowing the biggest dust bunnies off the shelves, and then wandered into her office.

Powering up her computer, Gail went online, surfing around and even checking fan fiction websites she read regularly, finding none with updates. No e-mails from friends or family to read or answer. Her day was too boring to qualify for a Facebook status update.

Leaving her office, Gail went back to the television. Glancing through her DVD and video collection, she found nothing appealing.

She tossed the remote onto the couch and got up to grab Butch for a quick walk around the block. The early evening air cleared her head, but gave her no ideas about how she could spend the long hours before bedtime.

Returning home, she went into the kitchen. After catching herself staring into the refrigerator for an unreasonably long period, Gail put her foot down. She was an adult, for goodness' sakes! Surely she could find something to do besides eat and mope around the house. It only took another thirty minutes of pointless wandering to accept that she could not.

Bored and desperate, she decided to head over to the hospital, thinking that perhaps Lily might be just as bored. It must be hard for her to go from being active to unable to move at all.

Stopping off at a Jamba Juice on her way, Gail purchased a smoothie, knowing Lily was allowed to have drinks, though not cleared yet for solid foods. During her visit yesterday afternoon, Lily had complained about wanting more than chalky milkshakes and the occasional juice box.

She regretted that she was not familiar enough with Lily's tastes to know if she would like the mango concoction, but carried the cup into the brightly lit hospital anyway. Reaching Lily's floor, she went to the room, pushed open the door, and stopped in her tracks.

The room seemed almost bursting with vibrantly healthy women. She could not even see the bed because of the crowd. She smiled and waited to be noticed, which did not take long.

The lively conversation came to a stop. As one, the women turned toward the door and stared at Gail with unfeigned interest.

"Er, hello," Gail said, feeling a bit like a mouse caught in an open field. "I'm Gail."

"Oh, sorry. Bad manners. Hello, I'm Cindy, and I'm a teammate of Lily's." The woman who spoke was a small blonde who wore her hair in a ponytail. "Do you know anyone here?"

When Gail told her no, Cindy quickly went around the room and introduced each of the women and gave her a little anecdote about them.

There were far too many names and faces for her to retain, but Gail smiled at each one of Lily's teammates. "It is good to meet you all."

"Hey, you work with Tiger, don't you?" one of the women asked.

"Lori, right?" Gail asked. At the nod, she asked, "Why do you call her Tiger?"

"Well, Lily just doesn't have quite the killer ring to it when shouted across the pitch."

Deirdre piped up, "Yeah. It's hard to intimidate our opponents when our toughest player has such a girlie name."

"I guess so." Gail laughed. She had thought since their disastrous introduction that Lily's name was far too feminine for such a hard-charging woman. It had always seemed that Lily was a little too raw and real to be named after a flower more associated with sweetness than ferocity.

"Your kid was under there with her, wasn't she?" Joan asked.

"Yes."

"Is she okay?"

"Yeah. In fact, she's in Santa Monica playing in a soccer tournament."

"Bitching!" Several women spoke in unison. They questioned her on Sierra's favorite position, the professional players she most admired, and how much she liked the beautiful game.

Tiffany asked, "Weren't you able to go down to watch?"

"I think she wanted a break from all the smothering I've been doing since the accident. It has been hard to let her out of my sight," Gail confessed.

"That must have been just awful for you." Angela reached out and patted her shoulder. "Thank goodness she's all right."

"Yeah. She was damned lucky."

"What position does she play?"

"Forward," Gail answered. She was hit by a flurry of questions about what school Sierra played for, how long she had been playing, and more. She enjoyed talking with these women about her daughter's soccer aspirations.

She jerked back slightly when a piece of paper was shoved at her. Glancing at it, she saw it was a spreadsheet. She looked up from the page in confusion into Tori's blue eyes. "Um?"

Tori laughed, "Wan said you might show up tonight. Here you go."

"What is it?"

"It's the team roster with all our phone numbers. We wanted to make sure you had a copy," Tori said.

"Um, thanks. Why are you giving it to me?"

"Wan told us that you've got Butch. If you need a break or anything, call any one of us, and we'll walk the dog or whatever."

"Oh, Butch has been no problem at all."

"Yeah, but adding a dog to your life can be challenging."

"She's been a great dog." Gail smiled. "My daughter just adores her."

"Yeah," Lorraine added. "A lot of the girls are jealous that you got the dog."

"That's only because we have to mow the lawn instead," joked Shira. "We've divided all Tiger's household chores up amongst ourselves. You get the fun stuff and we get the work."

Gail glanced toward the bed. The women blocked her view. "I'm sure Lily's very appreciative of your help."

"It's the least we can do. She's always been there for us," Caroline said, moving just far enough for Gail to see Lily.

Gail stepped further into the room and studied the still form. Lily looked healthier than she had two days ago. The bruising around her face had changed color from purple to yellow and green, but with the swelling going down, it was not nearly as frightening to look at her.

Her reverie was interrupted when Cindy cleared her throat. "Hey, did you hear the good news?"

"No. What?"

"Tiger had a series of neurological tests run today. She's got feeling and movement back in her feet and legs." Cindy touched Lily's hand lightly. "The doctors think that once the swelling in her spine goes down, she'll regain full range of motion."

"That's wonderful." Gail felt like a great weight had lifted off her shoulders.

"You bet it is," Caroline said.

"Damn right." Tori pumped her fist. "We weren't ready to start looking for a replacement keeper."

Furrowing her brow, Gail asked, "I'm sorry?"

"She's our goalkeeper and has a really low goals allowed percentage. We wouldn't want to go through our season without her."

"How soon is she going to be on her feet?" Gail asked. She had seen the wounds and remained skeptical that Lily might be playing anytime soon.

Tori replied, "A couple of months should do it."

"Yeah," Shira agreed. "We can take turns in the box until she can come back."

"Don't you think she'll need a lot longer to recover?" asked Gail. "I mean, her heart stopped for a while and she still can't move."

Lorraine disagreed. "She'll bounce back fast."

"Nothing keeps our girl down for long," added Joan. "Remember when she had pneumonia, and she still came out and played a killer game?"

The women laughed and began trading stories about the times Lily had played through the pain, which morphed into telling urban myths of local sporting legends taking one for the team.

Laughing at the story of the softball player who had broken her arm and still insisted on driving herself in her manual transmission car to the hospital, Gail tried to interject a little sanity into the discussion. "But aren't you afraid of a relapse? Bad things can happen long term when people push themselves too hard, too fast."

Joan waved her question off. "Even if she has to miss the rest of this season, she'll be fine by Ohio."

"Damn right. The games aren't until summer. That's nine months!" Tiffany exclaimed.

"Trust us." Tori looked down her nose at Gail. "We know her and it won't be a problem."

"Are you sure? There has got to be some serious physical therapy involved." Gail looked around the room. "I mean, she is still paralyzed."

"Not for long," Cindy replied. "The doctors said she'd regain full range of motion."

"Do they know that for a fact? One test might not tell the whole story."

"Yeah, but Lily's a machine," Joan answered. A couple of the women high-fived each other and bumped fists.

"See," said Tori. "You don't need to worry about Lil. Nothing keeps her down."

Gail could not believe these women were so oblivious. She worried they would pressure Lily into playing before she was ready. "I don't think it is in her best interest to be put into a position where she hurts herself because she doesn't want to let the team down. Sometimes those kinds of expectations can be really harmful to long-term recovery."

Joan narrowed her eyes and glared at Gail. "Look, I think we know Lily a little better than you do."

"Damn right we do."

Turning to the new speaker, Gail said, "Excuse me? Who are you?"

"I'm Alma." The small Latina woman tossed her hair over her shoulder and glared. "She talked about you some." Alma glanced at her teammates. "Remember how frustrated she would be sometimes? How she'd complain about the new woman at work? That was you, right?"

Gail blushed. "I admit we had our issues."

"Issues?" Shira scoffed. "From the stories she told, you were not very nice to her."

Knowing the truth of the accusation did not mean it hurt any less to hear a stranger say it. Gail sighed. "I realize that now." She looked into the faces of the women who meant so much to Lily. "I want to change that."

"Why?" Alma asked.

"Huh?" asked Gail.

"What made you suddenly want to be friends?"

"I reevaluated things. So many of our problems were just misunderstandings."

"Something must have happened to change your mind." Alma looked at her shrewdly. "Speaking for tigers, they don't usually change their stripes."

Gail forced herself to maintain eye contact. "My world was shaken when that building came down on my daughter. It only stabilized when both of them were brought out safely." Gail let her gaze move back to Lily. "I'm not the person I was before, and I'm hoping for a chance to let her see that."

"She doesn't need your pity. She'll be fine."

Gail felt like the conversation had spun out of control. "I don't pity her, Alma. I admire her." She ran her hand through her hair. "Everything I'm learning about her makes me want to know more. She was so brave when she was trapped in there with my daughter."

"So you're just grateful she helped your kid survive?"

"No. It is more than that. I really would like to be friends with her now."

"Well, you can't expect that Lily will just accept that you've turned over a new leaf," Cindy warned.

"I'm willing to give her all the time she needs."

"And maybe some space, too," Lorraine warned. "You have to realize that you two are not on the same page."

"Are you saying I shouldn't try?" Gail's eyes filled with tears.

"No. Just be patient. She's got a long recovery in front of her and she doesn't like being dependent on anyone." Caroline patted Lily's uninjured arm. "Being hurt like this will be tough for her. She will need help, but she won't be grateful to you for providing it."

Gail shook her head. "Why is she like that?"

"I blame her mother," Cindy answered.

"Yeah, it is always the mother's fault." Joan smirked at Gail. "No offense, of course."

Gail bared her teeth in a parody of a smile. "None taken, but there has to be more to it than that."

"Well, maybe when your family pulls their support away from you for no reason whatsoever and leaves you out in the cold to fend for yourself, you don't want anyone else to have that sort of power over you," Erica said sarcastically.

"And she doesn't need a…" Alma's statement was lost when a whimper came from the bed. Everyone turned their attention to the patient.

Lily groaned and slowly started to wake up. Her eyes moved behind her closed lids before finally cracking open. After a moment, she focused on the many faces around her. The slow smile she bestowed on the room caused the tension level to drop several degrees.

Without a word exchanged, the entire team ignored the previous discussion to concentrate on Lily, reaching out to touch her and speak soft greetings.

Gail was amazed at how gentle and careful the women acted toward Lily. Just a few moments ago they had been ferocious in her defense, but now they treated her like spun glass.

Lily coughed. Someone put a plastic cup to her lips. She grimaced at the taste of the tepid water. Coming forward, Gail offered the smoothie.

"Here, try this. It's mango," she said.

After taking a sip, Lily closed her eyes, evidently savoring the flavors. She opened her eyes and said, "More."

"There's no reason to get brain freeze." Gail brushed Lily's hair out of her face. "Take it slow and you'll get your fill."

"Trouble?" Lily mumbled around the straw clenched between her teeth.

Laughing, Gail said, "Don't worry. We'll say it was mine if the nurse has a problem."

With a slurping noise, Lily hit bottom and released the straw. She licked her lips and panted for a moment. When she regained her breath, she asked if her teammates had introduced themselves.

"Yes. I've met them all," Gail said.

"Good. I hope they've been nice."

"They've been fine. We were just getting to know each other."

"Hey, Tiger," Caroline said. "You didn't tell us Gail's kid played soccer."

"I don't recall having much opportunity to say much one way or another," Lily retorted. "You guys hardly let me get a word in edgewise."

Gail stood back and watched the women interacting with Lily. The teammates were obviously long-standing friends. She realized she felt jealous at how protective they were of Lily. It must be good to have such friends, she thought.

She had been very careful about friendships after her breakup. Sue's drinking had scared her and she had gotten used to hiding from people. Besides, taking care of her daughter and working full time hardly left a few minutes to read a magazine article, much less nurture a friendship. She wondered if she was doing the wrong thing by trying to change the relationship between herself and Lily. What could she offer someone who already had plenty of other people in her life?

Feeling tired and a little depressed, Gail excused herself and left Lily's room. She returned home and went into her bathroom to run a tub. When all else failed, a long soak always worked miracles on her mood.

She poured a couple of handfuls of perfumed sea salts and a few drops of essential oils into the water. Turning off the lights and lighting a few candles helped to create a calming atmosphere. She smiled as she slid into the water.

Her eyes closed and her fingers wandered along with her thoughts. Her hands massaged her legs. It had been a roller coaster of a day and the heat sinking into her skin made her think of sinking into another woman. She imagined someone else touching her, someone who wanted to make her feel good. Her hands traveled inward, stroking the soft skin of her inner thighs. She kept her touch innocent as long as possible until her skin felt super sensitized.

Not long afterward, she could no longer resist the throb of arousal. She parted her lower lips with two fingers. As her middle finger brushed against her clit, her hips rocked up in relief. She grazed her clit again and grabbed the edge of the tub with her other hand as her pleasure surged.

Gail rubbed her clit harder. Feeling the blood pounding between her legs, she knew she was close. She nearly went underwater when her orgasm hit. Only her firm grip on the lip of the tub saved her from a dunking.

Gasping, Gail let her head fall back as her breathing slowly returned to normal. She stayed soaking in the tub until her skin was wrinkly like a prune. Her muscles felt like jelly when she climbed out.

Barely able to stay awake to dry off completely, she got into bed and slid under the covers. For the first time since the accident, she slept through the night.

CHAPTER ELEVEN

Dr. Thea Patterson looked frazzled when she came into Lily's limited view. "Afternoon, Lily. How are you feeling?"

"Sore, but I'm a bit more awake today."

"Good to hear it. Let me look and see how things are healing." The doctor peeled back the gauze and ran a finger down the stitches on Lily's back. She cut through the bandage on Lily's head and examined that injury as well. "Not bad. I'm not seeing any infection."

"I feel a little warm."

"Your temperature is up, but that is your body's natural reaction to trauma. Your latest labs show your white cell count is up so I'm going to order blood and urine cultures to rule out an infection."

"Cool."

"All right. I'm going to test your sensation now."

"Okay, doc. When we're done, can I ask you questions?"

"Of course."

Dr. Patterson spent the next several minutes stabbing Lily with various instruments. She felt the pricks when the doctor finally reached areas that were no longer numb. For most of her lower back and legs, she felt some pressure but no pain, though she noticed she had more sensation today than she had felt before. She actually welcomed the pain because she knew it meant she was that much closer to walking again.

"Okay, what do you want to ask?" Dr. Patterson asked as she pulled off her gloves.

"First, how long? I mean, when will I be able to run again?"

"I can't give you an exact timetable. Part of your recovery will be based purely on your body's ability to heal. The other major factor is the effort and energy you are willing to put into your rehabilitation."

"But I can get back to where I was?"

"Not right away, but you should certainly regain full mobility. In any case, you will have a full and satisfying life."

"What about soccer?"

"I don't know. I can't realistically speak about that this early in your recovery. That being said, I don't expect you to have a permanent disability, but it could possibly take a year or longer before you can be competitive physically."

Lily was floored. When she had awakened and could not move, she had tried to accept that she might not walk again. Once the tests had revealed she would get better, she never figured her recovery would take so much time.

"Really?" she asked. "A year or two? That seems awfully long."

"Don't kid yourself. You're incredibly lucky. Not only did you survive a terrible accident, you also had good fortune in the way the building fell down around you. Heck, you could have been squashed like a bug. Instead, you'll be able to dance at your daughter's wedding."

"My daughter?"

"That cute little redhead who was in here the other day taking such good care of you."

"Oh, that was just the daughter of friend."

The doctor patted her on the arm. "Right," she said with a wink. "Friends."

Lily blushed, and did not understand why she reacted that way. Gail was just her co-worker, nothing else. They had just started to become friends. It did not mean anything that, of all the people who came to check on her, Gail was her most constant and consistent visitor. Or that she most looked forward to her visits.

Lily had just begun to drift off when she felt a shadow block the sunlight. Opening her eyes, she saw a strange man looming over her.

"Gah," she exclaimed, jerking awake. The action woke up the injuries on her back. She bit off a cry of pain.

"Oh, good. You're awake." The man pulled away the sheet covering her body.

Lily tried to grab at it, but she was stiff and still hurt too badly to move quickly. "Hey, who are you and what do you think you are doing?"

"I'm here to do a preliminary assessment for physical therapy."

"I wasn't told anything about this."

"This is standard treatment. Now, I need to check your range of motion."

"Wait a minute. I wasn't expecting a strange man to come in and start working on me with no warning."

"It is not my fault your care team hasn't informed you."

"No, but it is my body you're treating here." Lily took a deep breath and tried to calm down. "Let's start over. What's your name?"

"Bill."

"Well, Bill, I'm Lily. If you didn't know, I had a building fall on me last week. I don't think I'm actually up to physical therapy yet."

"Oh, no one expects you to be working on your own yet."

"Then why are you here?"

"As I said before, I need to conduct an assessment."

"Of what exactly?"

"I need to check how much mobility you have. I'll be moving your legs and arms to see what we can start with." He lifted her left leg and pushed her heel back toward her buttocks.

Lily could tell he was doing something to her lower body. She felt pulling on the stitches in her back, and suddenly remembered she was only wearing a hospital gown.

"Hey, dude. I'm feeling a little exposed."

"I'll be finished in a minute."

"During that minute, I'm lying here with my ass hanging out of this stupid gown. Shouldn't there be a nurse in here with you?"

"If you want one, we can schedule it. Let me assure you, I am strictly professional. Also, if we have to wait for a nurse to help, that will delay things even further."

"What's the almighty rush? It's not like I'm going anywhere."

"Oh, that's odd. That's not what my notes say."

"What is?"

"I just have a notation here that you're going to be transferred at the end of the week."

"Transferred?" Lily's heart started pounding. "What? Where?"

"I don't know. I could be reading this wrong." While Bill talked to her, he had continued to work on her legs. When he finished, he said brightly, "Now that wasn't so bad, was it? I'll just make these notes and be on my way. You have a nice day."

Left alone in the room, Lily stewed about the way Bill had treated her. Closing her eyes, she tried counting to ten. When that didn't work, she continued to count. At three thousand, one hundred and thirty-two, she heard a cough.

Opening her eyes, Lily saw an older woman wearing a bright yellow blouse sitting beside her bed.

"Yes?" Lily asked, squinting a little.

"Hello, I'm Theresa Robinson, your case manager. I hope this is a good time because I've got some paperwork for your upcoming transfer."

"What transfer? When the physical therapist mentioned it earlier, that was the first I'd heard of it."

"Oh, your doctor should have discussed it with you."

"Dr. Patterson didn't mention anything about it."

"I don't know what to tell you." Theresa shrugged. "Our facility is not designed for long-term care. We treat injuries, and then we have to move patients to other places for more specialized care."

"Why can't I go home?" Lily shifted on the bed. "I'll heal faster in my own bed."

"Most insurance companies will not pay for the level of in-home care you currently require. Until you've recuperated further, you would not be able to care for yourself." Theresa flipped through the paperwork she carried. "Now, we have two associated facilities for back injuries. One is in Orinda and the other is in San Mateo."

"What?" Lily could not believe what she heard. "There is nothing in the city?"

"None that are affiliated with us and approved by your insurance company."

"That's pretty far away. How long would I be there?"

"That would be entirely up to you. I understand the neurological tests have come back with positive results."

"Yeah, I'm definitely feeling something back there." Lily grimaced. "Right now, I've got a great, big pain in my ass."

"Good one. Humor is a definite sign that you are well on your way to recovery. So tell me, which facility is your preference?"

"Um…I don't know." Lily considered the number of visits she'd had lately. Few of her friends and colleagues would be able to travel so far to see her. She sighed. "All right. Let's do San Mateo."

"Excellent. Now if you would just sign these forms."

Lily was too tired to bother to read any of the small print. She just scrawled her signature where indicated on each of the forms.

"Very good. Thank you," said Theresa. She collected the papers and exited the room without a backward glance.

Alone again, Lily tried to sleep, but was too stressed from thinking about her morning visitors. Soon after she finally drifted off, she was awakened by the nurse taking her midday vitals. The nurse also turned on her television, but put the remote too far out of reach for her to turn it off, and left before she could make a protest.

The station was showing some sort of reality court show interrupted every few minutes by commercials for personal injury lawyers. Lily thought she would go mad from the constant hyping of who could get the most money from someone else's pain. It wasn't until another nurse came by that she was finally able to get the television shut down so she could hear herself think.

Thinking about her visitors, Lily wondered where Gail might be. She usually came to the hospital during the middle of the day and returned in the evening with Sierra. Thoughts of the precocious kid made her smile. Sierra would have her help with homework, and then she and Gail would sit and talk about anything and everything under the sun.

Their closeness did not have to mean anything, did it? Gail had mentioned she wanted to start over. She wanted to bury the hatchet. Lily had to admit that she liked the change. The anger was gone, but a new tension seemed to be creeping in.

She was shaken out of her contemplation when Gail flung herself into the room.

"What's up?" Lily asked.

"Oh, my day has been outrageous. I feel like a ping-pong ball." Gail sat down in the chair and began to talk about pieces of her day. She was always careful about confidentiality, but Lily stood high enough in the company's hierarchy to know most of the issues and players involved.

Their easy sharing was a pretty amazing thing, Lily mused. Just two weeks ago, no one would have expected her and Gail to carry on a conversation without resorting to bloodshed. Now they could chat for hours.

"Hey, am I boring you?" Gail asked.

"No, I just haven't gotten much rest today."

"Are you in pain?"

"No, just had a lot of visitors."

"Oh." Gail went quiet for a moment. "You don't want visitors?"

"No! God, no! My visitors are generally great and save me from death by boredom."

"What about today's visitors was different?"

"Oh, it was all the bureaucrats coming out of the woodwork now that I'm awake and coherent."

"Anything I can do to help?"

Lily automatically bristled. "No," she answered. "I can handle it."

"All right. I'm sure you can."

"Don't patronize me."

"I wasn't." Gail shook her head. "I'm just making things worse, aren't I?"

"Of course not."

"I guess I'll be going."

"Oh?"

"Yeah. I've got to get home. Sierra will probably want something other than takeout for dinner."

"I thought kids liked takeout."

"They might, but I feel guilty when it is for every meal." Gail shrugged. "I haven't been able to do the whole Domestic Goddess thing for a while."

Lily felt tears prickling her eyes. It was her fault Gail neglected her kid. "Yeah. You should go and be with her. She needs her mom."

"And she has me." Gail cocked her head. "Are you sure there wasn't something else you wanted to talk about?"

Shrugging slightly, Lily said, "I had someone in here talking about insurance and stuff."

"Just direct them to me. Everything will be handled by the worker's compensation carrier and out of any settlement from the tanker's insurance company. Not a single dime will come out of your pocket."

"Oh."

"Don't let them hassle you into signing anything. Feel free to direct them to my office and we'll handle it for you."

Even though she had felt overwhelmed by the paperwork earlier, Lily felt herself getting defensive. "I can take care of myself."

"I know you can, but there is no reason for you to also take care of the administrative bullshit or for you to go this alone. Once you get further along in your recovery and have a return to work date, make sure you get me all the required job accommodations."

"I'll just go back to working like normal."

"You can't know that yet. Your doctor may have you sitting more, and we'll want to make things as easy as possible for you to do your job until you're back at one hundred percent."

"What if I'm never back where I was?" Lily's voice rose on the last word. It was the first time she had spoken aloud about the possibility that she might not recover.

"Then we'll deal." Gail leaned forward. "You're good at your job. I'm confident we can find a way for you to do it, no matter the restrictions."

Lily grinned.

"What?"

"You just admitted I'm good at my job."

"Even when I was wasting so much time disliking you, I knew that!"

"Don't think for a minute I will forget you said that," Lily replied. She knew she wouldn't just remember Gail's compliment, but treasure it.

"You don't have to forget it. Just don't rub it in, unless you want your mango smoothie supply to dry up."

"Speaking of smoothies…"

"Sorry about that. Not only did I leave work late, but traffic was pretty bad, too."

"No worries. I'll just lay here in excruciating pain, smoothie-less."

"Okay, Bette Davis, shall I go get you one?"

"No, you need to get home. I'll just expect a bigger one tomorrow."

"I'll be happy to. Any requests?"

"Dealer's choice."

"All right. Have a good night." Gail casually kissed her fingers and pressed them to Lily's temple before heading out of the room.

Lily stiffened in surprise, unable to respond until the sound of Gail's footsteps faded. Lifting up her hand, she touched the place where Gail had touched her. The sign of affection seemed so natural and, truthfully, she liked that Gail had done it.

A few hours later, the nurse came in for a bandage change and to check her vitals. On her way out, she snapped off the light. With the visiting hours over, Lily was left to face the night alone. Thinking of Gail, she relaxed into pleasant dreams.

CHAPTER TWELVE

Gail left work early on Friday and headed over to the hospital after making a quick stop for another smoothie: strawberry and blueberry based, including some healing shots of immunity boosters and vitamins to improve the benefits.

Going into Lily's room, she was startled to find it empty. The cards and flowers were also gone. She felt a flash of fear that something horrible had happened, and went immediately to the nurse's station. No one was at the desk. She became more agitated the longer she had to wait.

"Finally," Gail said when a harried looking nurse passed by the station.

"May I help you, ma'am?"

"Yes. I was here to see the patient in room twenty eighteen."

The nurse thought for a moment, and then answered, "We don't have a patient in room twenty eighteen."

"Yesterday you did. She was there sleeping when I left last night. What happened to her and where is she now?"

"I'm sorry. I don't have that information."

"It is probably in your computer, though. Isn't it?"

"Oh, hospital policy is to never release information about our patients."

"If she's not in the room, she might not be a patient any more. That won't be violating your rules, would it?"

"Well, um…"

"Look, I'd like to know what happened to my friend. Could you please just look it up?"

"If she is your friend, why didn't she tell you?"

"I'm not going to debate this with you, especially as I don't know the answer to that question." Gail gritted her teeth and begged, "Could you just check on her status, please? Her name is Lily Rush."

The nurse spent a long moment considering the request before huffing and typing Lily's name into her computer. "Oh, she's been transferred to our San Mateo facility."

"What?"

"I said that she's been transferred…"

"I heard you. I don't understand what it means." Gail shook her head. "Why is she there? Did something happen?"

"No, nothing is wrong. It is just like moving a patient from the intensive care unit once they are stable. We only send off our patients once we know they are in the best shape to move."

"When did she go?"

"She left here this afternoon with the shuttle."

"You bused her down?"

"The shuttle is more like an ambulance. Our patients are treated properly. She should be nicely settled in by now."

"San Mateo, you said? Isn't that awfully far away?"

"It is one of the best facilities of its kind. It is also far better suited for rehabilitation."

"Why couldn't she do that here? It's nearer to her friends."

"We are not set up to give patients the physical therapy they need to return to full health."

"So she is really all right?"

"Yes. The notes state she's progressing really well. You should be pleased she's moving on to the next phase of her recovery."

"Do you have an address and a number where I can reach her?"

"Patients don't have phones in their rooms there." At Gail's glare, the nurse printed out the information for the long-term care facility. "Here is all you need to reach the floor nurse."

"Thank you."

In a daze, Gail left the hospital. She drove around the city for a while before turning her car to head home. Once there, she paced around her house. While she walked around in circles, she tried to figure out why Lily would just leave without saying anything. She had thought the two of them were really getting along.

Realizing she was working herself into a lather, she picked up the phone and called Wan. The call went to voice mail. She continued pacing around the house, waiting for him to call back.

When Sierra came home, she tried to put the day's disturbance aside to focus on getting dinner ready and making sure homework was done. Sierra seemed to sense her unease, and she went upstairs to work on her Spanish vocabulary without a complaint.

Gail went back to pacing. When her phone finally rang, she nearly broke her neck diving to pick it up. "Yes? Hello?"

"Hey, Gail. It's Wan. I got your message."

"Yeah, did you know Lily was moved?"

"When I went over this morning, they were making the final arrangements."

"Why didn't she tell me?"

"If it is any consolation, she didn't tell anyone. Honestly, I don't think she expected it to happen so fast. I mean, she only woke up ten days ago last Sunday." He sighed. "She's also pretty private and very used to handling things on her own. You shouldn't take it personally."

"Are you going to see her?"

"Yeah, I'll drive down tomorrow to make sure she is settling in all right."

"How long will she be there?"

"Probably a month."

"That long?"

"It will be at least that long until she can take care of herself. The therapy will be pretty intense, but Lily is darned motivated to get back on her feet."

"I'm not sure when I'll be able to get down there," Gail said. "It is so far, and I've got work and all of Sierra's obligations."

"Don't worry. I'll tell her you're thinking of her."

The sentiment seemed inadequate, but Gail cleared her throat and replied. "Thank you. Um, could you please give her my number, too? I'll also see about getting down there next week, and she can let me know if she needs me to bring anything, or if she's bored or anything."

Wan said, "I'll tell her. I know she didn't mean anything by not telling you about the transfer. She has a hard time reaching out at the best of times and this whole injury thing has thrown her for a loop."

"I know. It's just a shock, you know. I thought we...well, I'm not sure what I thought."

"I understand." Wan paused. "Don't give up on her, okay? She's a tough nut on the outside, but well worth the trouble of breaking through her shell."

"But does she want me to get inside? I want to be her friend, but I don't want to force a friendship on her."

"I don't know what to tell you. Why don't you ask her yourself when you see her?"

"Yeah, I guess I'll do that." Gail sighed. "Thanks, Wan. You're a real pal."

"Thank you. Thank you very much," he replied, mimicking Elvis Presley's distinctive voice. "The king has now left the conversation."

Gail laughed. "All right. Goodbye."

Feeling a little better after having spoken to Wan, Gail hung up the phone and began doing all the small tasks around the house that had fallen through the cracks during the past couple of weeks.

She filled up her entire weekend with chores and chauffeur's duty. Sierra had a number of commitments over the weekend that sent them traveling back and forth across the Bay Bridge. She thought about Lily often, but made it through the hours by keeping busy.

Gail finally made arrangements for Sierra to go to a friend's house after soccer practice on Tuesday. She thought she could manage to leave work early and make the drive to San Mateo, and was pleased when the plan came together. She hoped the rehabilitation center's visiting hours were the same as the hospital's since she wanted a chance to spend some quality time with Lily.

As she drove to San Mateo, she wondered how Lily filled her days. She had not heard of her asking for any work but then again, being the distribution director was a lot more hands on than the other director level positions.

After getting off the 101, she made a couple of wrong turns before she finally found the right building. A very helpful woman at the desk told her Lily was receiving physical therapy, but she was welcome to observe.

"That would be great. Thank you," Gail said.

She followed one of the aides to a large, brightly lit area, so happy to see Lily across the room that she barely remembered to thank the woman for being her guide.

About to start across the floor toward Lily and a white uniformed man standing beside her, she stopped in shock when Lily's hand slipped from the rail. Without the safety belt attached to her waist and a winch above her head, Lily would have hit the floor.

"Clumsy," said the heavyset man.

Gail snapped from visually checking to make sure that Lily was all right to glaring at the man standing in front of her.

"You're wasting my time," he said. "Now get up and finish the exercise."

Lily said nothing. She just pulled herself upright with great effort and began a walking motion. Her legs swung forward. It looked ungainly, but Gail was surprised to see so much change in so few days. She smiled in relief at seeing so much function returning until she heard the man speak again.

"Move faster. I swear I've never seen anyone more pathetic." He spat into a cup. "It makes me sick that I have to work with someone so lazy. Wake up and put in an effort."

"I am trying." Lily was shaking and panting from exertion, trying to get her body to obey.

"Not good enough. You ever want to get out of here, you'll work harder." He put a hand on his crotch and adjusted himself. "Of course, maybe you're putting off getting better because you really want a piece of this."

"Don't flatter yourself. I'd sooner eat glass." Lily made it to the end of the parallel bars. "Now what?"

"You walk back, fall into your little chair, and go back to your room."

"We're done then?"

"Yep. You get to go have a good cry, and I get to work with people who actually care about getting better."

Gail grew furious hearing his abuse, but she was afraid to step forward. If she confronted him and he retaliated, Lily would be the one to suffer. She backed out of the room and went back to the lobby to ask for directions to Lily's room.

"She hard at work?" the receptionist asked.

"Something like that." Gail shifted her bag to her other hand. She had brought some cookies that Sierra had baked and a few other things she hoped Lily might like.

"The residences are just down that hall and up one floor. There is an elevator and a set of stairs. She's in room 360."

"Thank you." Gail slowly walked to the room, distressed by how bare it seemed. All the cards from the hospital were in a pile on the dresser and there were no flowers.

Afraid she might be caught spying, Gail left and went to a small waiting room down the hall, occupied by three people in wheelchairs in front of a television watching a fishing show. None of them turned to look at her or acknowledge her in anyway.

The show did not hold her attention, so Gail stared out the window at the grounds. There was very little grass, mainly dirt and spindly trees filled the spaces between the building and the parking lot. She felt depressed, which wasn't alleviated by knowing she could leave in a few hours.

Hearing a noise, she turned to see Lily using a manual wheelchair to propel herself down the hallway. Her hair was plastered to her head from her workout. She didn't glance up.

Waiting a moment, Gail followed her into her room, where Lily was wobbling in her effort to maneuver onto the bed.

"May I help?" she asked.

Startled, Lily nearly fell over. "What? Oh, Gail. I didn't expect anyone to be there."

"I am and I'm offering."

Lily gritted her teeth and managed to get onto the bed to lie down. She used her arms to move herself into a more comfortable position against the pillows. "When did you get here?"

"About a half hour ago."

"What did you see?"

"A sadistic bastard and a miracle. I didn't think you'd be walking again so soon."

"If you can call that walking."

"For someone whose back looked crushed when I first saw you in intensive care, I'd say that looked remarkably like walking to me." Gail came closer. "I'm so impressed."

Lily shrugged and shifted on the bed. "I could be further along."

"What, according to that jerk? I think he should be reported for abuse."

"He's not so bad."

"Compared to what? Josef Mengele?"

"I need someone to push me. If I didn't, I'd still be laying on my stomach, pissing and moaning."

"There is a difference between pushing and abuse. He should be reported."

"No. I can handle this myself. If nothing else, he is giving me an incentive to get out of here as soon as I can."

Gail bit her tongue. She could not believe Lily was so complacent about accepting the physical therapist's rude treatment. She also knew she was not going to win this argument with the stubborn woman.

Changing the subject, she asked, "How are things otherwise?"

"Not bad."

"You get many visitors?"

"Most of the team came down this weekend. It was good to see them all."

"Sierra was busy or we would have come."

"I know," Lily said quickly.

"She made these cookies for you, though." Gail pulled a plastic bag from her satchel. "She did three different kinds, so you would have a good selection."

Tears glistened in Lily's eyes. "Thanks. You should thank her for me. They look great."

"She misses you and wanted to come down, but it is a little hard to get here."

"I know."

"Why didn't you say anything?" Gail asked after a moment.

"About what?"

"About being moved way the hell and gone down here."

"Why would I?"

"I think getting a transfer would come up in conversation."

"It obviously didn't."

Gail pinched the bridge of her nose. "I would have liked to known."

"Why?" Lily seemed confused.

"It was frightening to come into the hospital, see the empty bed where you had been, and not know what had happened to you."

"I'm sorry. I didn't think it was anybody's business but my own."

"I thought we were friends."

"We are getting more friendly, sure."

"So friends tell each other things that impact their lives."

"I don't need your permission."

"That's not what I mean and you know it. My wanting to know what's going on does not mean I want to control you."

"Don't you think I know that?"

"Honestly? I don't. You expect me to act a certain way and I'm sorry, but I'm not going to be like the other people in your life who have let you down," Gail said earnestly.

"I'm trying."

"You want to tell me what you're thinking right now?"

"I don't understand why you're being so nice."

Gail had to stop herself from laughing at the petulant tone. Lily sounded a lot like Sierra just then. "I owe you everything. You saved my daughter's life."

"Anybody would have done the same. There is no debt to repay for that."

"Then what about for how I treated you before all this? I have a lot of things to make up to you." Gail leaned closer to Lily. "Please let us be friends."

"What if I said I don't need any more friends?"

"Everyone can use another friend. It is the only thing in life where moderation is not necessarily the best thing."

"I'm fine as I am. You've got plenty of other things to do instead of worrying about me."

"I don't like worrying about you, but I do like thinking about you." Smiling, Gail added, "Even before all this, I thought about you a lot."

"You did?"

"Yeah. I think we got off on the wrong foot and…"

"Wrong foot?" Lily laughed. "We couldn't be in the same room without arguing."

"Is that what either of us wanted to do? Or was it expected?" Gail thought out loud. "When you were rude on the first day, it set up a pattern where we both attributed the worst to explain the other's behavior."

"I was busy! You never seemed to understand that I'm not ignoring you for the fun of it. I've got thousand-ton ships that cost hundreds of dollars every minute they aren't moving. I can't just stop and write a progressive discipline memo when I've got shipments incoming and outgoing."

"See, that's what I'm talking about. I didn't mean for you to drop everything when I talked about documenting poor behavior. We never explained ourselves. I'm sorry. I know better now and will be more respectful of your job."

Lily blinked at her.

"Can you forgive me? Can we move past this?"

"I guess." Lily bit her lip. "I guess part of me wonders why you're pushing this, though."

"Because I was wrong about you," Gail admitted. "I talked to Sierra. You not only saved her life, you kept her sane. She had no idea how badly you were hurt. You talked to her and calmed her down." She sat down on the side of the bed. "I spoke to the EMTs.

You told them to take her first so she wouldn't have anything else to have nightmares about."

"She's a good kid. She didn't deserve to suffer any more than she already had."

"I was so sure you didn't give a tinker's damn for me and mine, yet you nearly died saving Sierra. I was obviously wrong about you. I couldn't live with myself if I didn't make amends for my past actions and make every effort to get to know the real you."

Lily aborted an attempted shrug with a hiss.

Gail winced in sympathy as Lily struggled to roll over onto her stomach. She reached out with both hand and began lightly massaging Lily's tense back. "Please let me be here for you."

"I don't want to need you," Lily mumbled into her pillow.

"What about what I need?"

Lily took a breath, but was saved from answering by the arrival of a nurse, who bustled in with a change of clothes and ordered Gail to leave the room.

Quietly, Gail waited outside.

"I've given her a shot, so you'd better go on in and finish up your conversation," the nurse said when she exited the room.

"Thanks," Gail replied. She wanted to ask how Lily was really doing, but feared Lily would fall asleep if she delayed too long.

Lily was dozing when Gail approached the bed. She could tell from her relaxed state that the drugs were delivering their promised relief.

"I'm sorry I was such a bitch," Lily mumbled into the pillow.

"Was?" Gail laughed. "Don't worry. You are in pain, but you also have a point. I shouldn't expect you to trust me yet."

"Yet?"

"Yes. You haven't seen the last of me. I've managed to get my foot through the door and I'm not going to give up now." She squeezed Lily's hand. "You couldn't blast me out of your life with dynamite."

"What about rudeness and generally boorishness?"

"Those work better, but you'll have to step up your game if you think that will be enough. Remember, I deal with the likes of Ken every day. If I can take him, I can take you."

Lily's eyes started to close. She blinked owlishly. "I didn't say it before, but thanks for coming. I...uh...I liked seeing you."

"Good. Because I'll be back and I'll be bringing Sierra. She misses you."

"Miss her, too," murmured Lily as she fell asleep.

Gail watched Lily sleep for a while before unpacking the rest of the gifts, which included several magazines and a couple of brainteaser collections. Pressing her kissed fingertips to Lily's temple, she left to make the long drive home, hopeful that she and Lily were finally moving beyond their initial antagonism.

CHAPTER THIRTEEN

Lily opened her eyes. Hearing a repeating squeaking noise in the hall, she recognized it as the left rear wheel of the food cart being pushed down the hallway. She turned her head and looked at the pale sunlight streaming through the blinds.

She knew the cart would not stop at her room. The facility practiced a version of tough love with regard to many of its services. Once the physical therapists had determined she was able to maneuver on her own, they began to require it.

She now had to dress herself and make it to the cafeteria if she wanted to eat breakfast or any other meal. The food was bland and it was that, almost more than being able to walk again, that drove her to push her recuperation.

In her twenty years in San Francisco, she had gotten very spoiled about the progressive political atmosphere, the weather, the easy acceptance of her sexual orientation and, most especially, the food. She loved the variety and the spiciness that the mélange of cultures brought to her life and to her taste buds. She missed the taste of fresh food.

With a sigh, she flung the covers off and reached for the bar hanging over her bed. Making sure she had a good grip, she pulled herself upright. The muscles pulled in her lower back as she worked her legs over to the side. Taking a deep breath, she gave a final heave and sat upright on the edge of the bed.

She pulled the walker closer, and leaning heavily on it, stood up. Moving slowly, her legs still dragging a little, she made it to the bathroom. After using the safety bars to help ease her way to the seat, she stared at them.

Her house had nothing like that. She wanted so badly to be gone from here, but had to admit to herself she was not ready to return to life as it was before. She slapped her thighs, gratified to feel the brief pain of the blow. While sensation had returned, she still had problems getting her legs to do what she wanted, which she found very frustrating.

Besides the occasional cramps that curled her toes, she also suffered intermittent paralysis. Inexplicably, her legs would just stop responding to the messages from her brain. It was maddening. And there was the pain in her back. No bones had been broken, but that was a mixed blessing as damaged soft tissues and tendons took longer to heal.

Scooting over to the sink, she brushed her teeth, and stared at herself in the mirror as she moved the toothbrush up and down. The bruises and scratches on her face had faded, and her dark hair had grown in since the emergency room doctor had shaved it to access her head wound.

Bending over to spit out the toothpaste, Lily winced. Carefully standing upright, she noticed new lines of pain on her face. Moving her mouth and blinking helped remove the signs of suffering. She resolved to continue her facial relaxation exercises when Gail and Sierra visited. She did not like to show pain, and did not want the visits from her two newest friends marred by them fussing over her.

At a snail's pace, she moved to the closet and dressed in pants and a button-down shirt, sweating slightly when she finished tucking it in. She could not stop to rest. Gail was bringing Sierra over before lunch and she was not about to inflict a meal in the cafeteria on them. But if she were going to skip lunch, she needed to eat something before they arrived.

Today, she sat back on the bed to put on her shoes. Generally, she wore a pair of slippers or slid her feet into loafers. In honor of her expected visitors, she wanted to put on a pair of shoes with laces that tied, which proved one of the hardest tasks of the day. Getting her leg up high enough and her foot at the right angle was a chore, but the result was worth it, she thought. She no longer looked or felt like an invalid.

Lily used the walker on the long march from her room to the cafeteria. She nodded at the residents she passed. Many of the quadriplegics had been simply rolled into the hallway in their wheelchairs after they were assisted with dressing and eating.

She ate the runny scrambled eggs and toast, and gulped down several glasses of metallic tasting orange juice. After leaving the cafeteria, she went to the weight room to begin a session of self-directed exercises. She was willing to do almost anything to get her strength back, which included working out as often as she could.

Returning to her room, she changed out of her damp shirt and sat by the window to quietly wait for her visitors to arrive.

She heard Sierra long before the girl burst into her room and exclaimed, "Lily, Mom said you'll be coming back to the city soon."

Nodding, she said, "Yeah, I'll be back by the end of the week."

"That's so cool. We'll be able to see you all the time, then." Sierra sat down on the bed. "Won't that be great?"

"Lily will need a chance to get settled back into things," Gail said, coming into the room. "It might be a few days before we're able to visit."

"But what about Butch?" Sierra asked.

Lily looked up. "What about her?"

"You'll need help walking her, won't you?"

She wanted to disagree, but knew the powerful dog could easily pull her off her feet in her current physical condition. She smiled with her teeth clenched and said, "Yeah. I'll need you to help me take care of her."

She saw Gail smile and started to get defensive. Taking a breath, she thought for a moment, trying to let the anger go. She knew Gail wasn't judging or pitying her. Sighing, she asked, "How has the beast been?"

"She's the greatest dog ever!" Sierra said.

"You're telling me. My dog is perfect."

"Right," Gail scoffed. "That perfect dog ate an entire loaf of bread."

Lily blushed. "She is a bit of a bread hog."

"There were dog bones on the counter next to the bread that she didn't touch at all. I don't understand it."

"Oh, she knows better than to take treats that haven't been offered to her. Bread, on the other hand, is fair game." Lily shrugged. "I don't know where the need comes from but she digs any kind she can get her teeth into."

"A little warning would have been nice."

"Oh, where's the fun in that?" Lily smiled.

Sierra tugged on Lily's arm. "Guess what?"

"What, Sierra?"

"We brought you something."

"Really?" Lily looked at Gail. "It isn't a grocery bill for bread, is it?"

"No, silly." Jumping off the bed, Sierra went to get the bag that Gail held out. "I made...I mean, we made you brownies." She glanced at her mother.

"Thank you both. I really appreciate you bringing me them since I'm starting to forget what good food tastes like."

"Is it that bad?" Sierra asked.

"Worse." Lily wondered if it would be rude for her to tear into the brownies right away.

"I'm sorry to hear that," Gail said. "I guess that means you'll be happy to know that we got permission to take you out to lunch."

Lily looked up from wrestling with the rather tightly wrapped plate of brownies. "Really?"

"Yep. We can go to one of the places next to the freeway exit. I'm sorry we can't go further, but we were only able to spring you for two hours."

Lily beamed. "No, that's great. I'll take McDonald's if necessary to avoid another meal here." She looked at the walker and lost her smile.

"What's wrong?"

"Um…I don't know if I'm going to be able to do this."

"We'll work it out. I think you'll be able to just slide into the seat of my CR-V."

Lily did not feel sure, but she wanted so badly to be out of the facility even for a little while, she was willing to try walking. Since Sierra and Gail had started coming regularly, she rarely moved at all during their visits because she did not want them to see her pain or her ungainly efforts to make her legs work.

She climbed to her feet with a sigh, shuffled to the walker, and used it to help her turn and head toward the door.

Sierra came up beside her. "How does that work?"

"I lean on it and my legs don't have to take all my weight." Talking about what she was doing actually helped Lily take her mind off the effort. "Unlike crutches that take weight off your foot, the walker just supports me so I don't fall down."

"Does it hurt?"

"Only when I laugh."

"You have such a lovely laugh," Gail said.

Lily raised an eyebrow. "I haven't had much to laugh about in here."

"I make you laugh, don't I?" Sierra asked.

"Yeah." Lily started to make her way down the hallway. "You do. Thank you for reminding me."

At the car, Lily accepted Gail's help. The effort to make it to the parking lot had taken most of her energy and she was glad to sit down again. She concentrated on not crying or throwing up. She enjoyed being idolized by Sierra and did not want to ruin things by breaking down and screaming in pain.

Gail leaned across the space between the seats. "She would think even more of you."

"What?"

"If you showed Sierra that you were hurt and allowed her assistance. I don't think there's anything that would please her more than helping you."

Lily looked deep into Gail's green eyes. "How did you know?"

"You wear some of your feelings on your face."

"I thought I had been practicing enough."

"Practicing?" Gail asked as she pulled out from the parking space.

"Yeah. I worked out in front of the mirror to not show so much pain," Lily confessed. "I don't want you to feel sorry for me."

Gail accelerated the car onto the busy street. "For the record, neither of us pities you. I'm actually amazed by you. Every time we visit, you've regained more mobility."

"I'm going to do my story on you," Sierra said from the backseat.

Lily started to shift in her seat toward Sierra, but stopped with a groan. "What story?" she forced out from between clenched teeth.

"For my journalism class I have to interview someone I admire. I'm going to do you."

"Perhaps you should ask Lily if it is okay," Gail admonished Sierra. "She might not want to be the subject of your story."

For a moment, Lily couldn't speak past the lump in her throat. "It would be my pleasure."

Gail reached over and squeezed Lily's knee. "Thank you."

"Are you still going to be thankful when I point out you just drove by the restaurant?"

"What?" Gail glanced into the rearview mirror. "Shit."

"Mom, you cussed," Sierra pointed out.

"I know, sweetie, and I'll put a quarter in the jar when we get home."

"Jar? Quarter?" Lily asked.

"It is a swear jar and it has really helped both of us reduce our potty mouths."

"Sounds like a good idea. Of course, I'd be bankrupt after a single session with my physical therapist."

"Well, I've seen that guy and I'd be doing more than swearing at him. He should have his license pulled."

"You've got to admit his manner, while brutal and unorthodox, has certainly been an incentive for me to get better." Lily grimaced when the car went over a speed bump in the parking lot. "I don't think I'd be in any shape to go home without his abuse."

"Well, I am glad for that."

"Oh?"

"Yeah, I miss you when I'm at work. Since you've been in this facility, I haven't been able to see you regularly." Gail pulled the car into a parking space.

Sierra said, "I didn't know you before, but I miss you, too."

"Thanks, kid, and thank you." Lily allowed Gail to help her out of the car.

"Don't mention it. It has been my pleasure to get to know you."

Lily could not help the blush heating her cheeks. "Me, too." She stopped in the doorway of the restaurant and sniffed in pleasure. "Oh, my."

"Good?"

"Food that actually smells like food." Lily grabbed a menu as soon as she sat down. She suddenly glanced up in alarm. "I don't have any money."

"No problem. I'll get this."

"Thanks." Lily flipped the pages to the sandwiches, trying to find something from the cheapest section of the menu.

Gail reached across the table and laid her warm fingers on Lily's wrist. "Order want you want. You can always pay me back by taking me out to a fabulously expensive meal when you're back in the city."

"Like a date?" Her voice rose on the last word. Lily cursed silently.

"Um, maybe...uh...maybe like friends who might someday... someday soon be more than friends." Gail pushed a lock of hair behind her ear. "Would you want to be something like that?"

Lily surreptitiously wiped her palms on her slacks and looked back down at her menu. "I'm not sure."

"Is it a problem that I'm thinking of you as more than just a friend?"

"Problem? No! No, it's not a problem for me." Lily lifted her gaze to look at Gail.

"Good." Gail smiled. "I'd kind of like that."

Lily stared into Gail's eyes, and the rest of the world disappeared.

"Man," Sierra interrupted.

Gail turned to regard her daughter. "What, Sierra?"

"Adults are weird."

Lily laughed. "Tell me something I don't know."

"I bet you don't know that when you two were looking all lovey-dovey at each other, the waitress came by and left," Sierra replied.

"No!" Lily exclaimed. "We need to order."

Gail grinned and caught the server's eye. "Don't worry. We'll get you fed. No one goes away from my table hungry."

"Good to know." Lily felt herself flushing. "I'll keep that in mind."

CHAPTER FOURTEEN

"I'm glad you're here," Lily said without looking up, busily rolling back and forth in her wheelchair in the middle of the room. The wheels squeaked loudly when she turned.

"What's with the chair? I thought you were walking okay now," Wan said.

"Policy. I've got to leave in the wheelchair."

Wan smiled. "I take it you're ready to go?"

"Oh, yeah."

"What do I need to do?"

"I'm still waiting for the last bit of paperwork they're insisting I sign before I can be released, but that stuff there," Lily pointed at a small pile of belongings on the bed and the walker beside it, "that is the stuff that needs to go in your car. Think it will fit?"

"My car isn't that small." Wan sniffed. "We can always put the stuff on your lap."

"I expected as much." Snapping her fingers, Lily ordered, "We're burning daylight. Get this stuff moving."

Wan tugged on his bangs and picked up the box. "You just had me come down here for my strong back."

"It surely wasn't for your smart mouth." Lily grinned. "Have I told you lately how much I appreciate you coming to get me?"

"Yep," Wan replied. "I could stand to hear it again, though."

"Thank you." She popped a wheelie, and then spun the chair around in a circle. "If you didn't come and get me, I'd be stuck here for two more days."

"Why? I thought you were cleared to go?"

"Oh, I am, but I still can't drive, and the next shuttle I can get a seat on won't be until Tuesday."

"That just seems mean."

"You're telling me. I felt like they pulled the rug out from under my feet when they told me that."

Wan walked over and squatted down beside the chair. "I know it must have been hard for you to call me."

Blushing, Lily looked away. "It nearly killed me," she whispered.

"But you did it anyway."

"I couldn't stand staying here even more."

"Sometimes, grasshopper, that is the way we grow. We are forced to make a choice between the hard and the even harder."

"Making a choice between two evils?"

"Well, asking for help is something you've never done before, but it is never evil."

"You say that now."

"I've said that always. I know you've had a tough time, but you make it harder on yourself when you won't reach out to your friends."

"I don't like owing people."

"Friends don't count the cost. There is no calculus involved. You just do what needs doing."

"That doesn't always work."

"No, but it works more often than not." Wan sighed. "I wish you could trust that we're here for you."

"I know. I'm trying to do better."

"Yes, you are." He ruffled her hair. "I'm proud of you."

"So have I built enough character yet?" Lily asked, sticking her lip out in a pout.

"Yeah. I'll put in a good word for you to make sure your karmic debt has been paid off." Wan walked back to the pile of stuff. "I expect you to keep working on this, though."

"What do you mean?"

"Well, there have been some changes at your house."

"What?" Lily demanded, frightened at what strangers might have done to her home. "What's happened?"

"Your teammates wanted to do something that would help you handle living on your own." Wan smiled. "They got an accommodation consultant and made some renovations last week."

"Like what?"

"Things like safety bars in the bathroom and around a new, adjustable bed. I think you'll be pleased, and I hope you'll remember to thank them even if you're not."

"Yes, sir. I'll be good."

"Glad to hear it. Let me get this stuff into the car and maybe the nurse will come with the paperwork."

"From your lips to their ears."

While Wan carried the boxes out, Lily paced. More accurately, she rolled the wheelchair back and forth across the room. While she had to admit that the chair was pretty responsive, she felt ecstatic that she was not confined to one permanently.

Finally, the floor nurse came into the room. "Ms. Rush. I have your paperwork here."

"Great. Let me just sign what I need to and you can have the room back."

"We aren't quite so busy that we need to throw you out."

"Don't take it personally, but I'm happy to be getting out of here."

"I understand that. I bet you're missing your home."

"And the rest of my life." Lily smiled. "I miss my job and my dog, and I miss doing the things I used to do."

"Don't push yourself too hard getting back into everything.

You can't expect to just step back into your life at the same level you were at before the accident."

"I know."

"Intellectually, you may know that, but it is an entire other thing when you're in it." The nurse handed her a clipboard. "Initial every highlighted line and sign these three places."

"Sure thing."

Wan returned and smiled at the nurse. "Oh, good. She was chomping at the bit to get those completed."

"Indeed." The nurse held out a small paper bag. "Here are her current medications."

Lily looked up. "I'll take those."

"Of course."

Trying to hide his smile, Wan left with the final load of belongings.

"There. Was there anything else?" asked Lily when she handed back the forms.

"You need to keep your copies. Did the physical therapist give you the list of exercises?"

"Yes. They're with my other things."

"Good. Here is an appointment card with a physical therapist. They will see you three times a week for the next ninety days."

"You aren't expecting me to come back here, are you?"

"Oh, no. The facility we've contacted for you is the one nearest your office. If you don't like them, I'm sure your worker's compensation carrier will have plenty of other options."

"Okay."

"As I mentioned before, these are your medications. There are refills on the pain medications."

"Great. Anything else?"

"Yes. Here is a membership card for a fitness center with many locations in the city."

"That's cool."

"That is it. I won't keep you any longer."

"Thanks." Lily waggled her wheelchair chair from side to side. "I mean it. You all did a good job on getting me back in shape as quickly as you did. I know that some of it might be wanting to get rid of me, but I do appreciate it."

"You did the really hard work. We just gave you the impetus."

"Thanks."

"Just don't think you're done yet. You can't take it easy, and you won't be who you were unless you keep up with the exercises."

"I know." Lily started to roll toward the door. "Take care."

"You, too."

Lily propelled the wheelchair down the hallway, toward the exit and freedom. She barely spared a smile for the good wishes called her way from patients who had been at the facility before she arrived and would probably stay long after she left.

When she hit the sunshine outdoors, she let the wheelchair coast to a stop. She set the brake and looked at Wan leaning against his car.

"You ready to blow this Popsicle stand?" he asked.

"You bet. Could you slide the walker over this way?"

"I thought you could walk without assistance."

"For short distances, yeah, but I'm not going to give anyone the satisfaction of seeing me fall on my ass before I even make it out of the parking lot."

"Gotcha."

Lily swung the footplates out of the way and gingerly stood up. She leaned on the walker, grinning at Wan. "You can let go now."

"Oh, okay."

She walked the final steps to the curb and the parked car. Getting into his sports car was a lot harder than climbing into Gail's SUV. She grimaced as the muscles in her back pulled.

"You ready?" he asked.

"You bet."

Wan folded the walker and managed to wedge it into the backseat. "All right. We're off to your place with no stopping."

"Thanks." Lily flipped down the visor and lifted up the cover over the vanity mirror. She adjusted it so she could watch the facility disappear into the distance. "None too soon."

"What was that?"

"I was just saying I'm glad to be out of there. I can't wait to sleep in my own bed."

"You going to have any problems with the stairs?" Wan glanced at her. "They knew you weren't in a wheelchair, so they didn't put ramps up."

"I'll manage."

"Of course you will."

"I might have to sleep on the couch for a night or two."

"How is that going to be on your back?"

"I'll survive. The bed I've been sleeping on wasn't the best in the world."

"Can't imagine hospital beds are that comfortable."

"That's why they keep the patients as drugged up as they do. They don't want us screaming in agony." She sighed. "It will be a pain to get my groceries, though."

"Oh, I wouldn't worry about that yet."

Lily looked suspiciously at him. "What do you mean?"

"Just that your team filled your fridge and freezer while they were at it."

"Filled it with what?"

"Food, silly."

"How do they know what kind of food to get?"

"Well, they cleaned out the fridge, so a lot of it was just replacing what had spoiled." Wan easily shifted the car on the highway. "They also bought some frozen dinners. A few of the more daring members actually made casseroles."

"Wow. They did that for me?"

"Yep."

"How am I going to repay them?"

"By being a friend. They are doing everything in their power to make your recovery as painless as possible. You won't need to worry about mowing the lawn or anything else." Wan moved into the passing lane and pressed on the accelerator. "When are you going to get your pooch back?"

"I don't know." Picking at a thread on her pants, Lily added, "It's going to be hard to walk her for a while."

Wan snorted. "You're telling me. You are certainly not steady enough on your pins to trust her on a leash."

"Butch isn't that bad."

"I didn't say she was bad. She's just a big dog with a lot of energy." Continuing to accelerate, Wan passed several cars as if they were standing still. "Sierra just loves her."

"So I've heard."

"Jealous much?"

Lily shrugged. "Butch has always been just my dog. This is the longest we've ever been apart." She went quiet for a few minutes. "What if she doesn't remember me?"

"Oh, she will. You're not easily forgotten and you're her momma."

"I guess."

"I'm sure Gail would be happy to bring her over tonight."

"I can't ask her to do that."

"Does she even know you're going to be back at your house today?"

"She knew I was getting back this weekend."

"Why didn't you call her?"

"Why should I?"

"I could be mistaken, but I feel that the two of you have something brewing." Wan glanced at her. "Am I wrong?"

"No," Lily answered shortly.

"Then why didn't you let her know you were being released? Or better yet, ask her to pick you up? I would have thought Gail read you the riot act after you left the hospital without telling her."

Lily laughed. "She sure was mad, wasn't she?"

"I think she was more hurt than mad. She cares about you."

"Does she really?"

"Hasn't she shown that? I mean, anyone willing makes this drive as often as she did must truly like you."

"It's just hard for me to wrap my head around it. I woke up and so much was changed."

"Do you care about her at all?"

"Of course. She's been great." Lily stared at the rapidly approaching city skyline. She had never been so grateful to see the familiar sight of the Bank of America building. "I don't know what I would have done without her."

"Then why does it look like you are going to hurt her again?"

Sighing, Lily said, "I'll call her when I get home."

"I'm not trying to force you to do anything you don't want to do. I also don't want you to lose something because you were scared."

"I'm not scared."

"Really? Then what is keeping you from opening up to her?"

"It's too soon."

"Too soon for what? You broke up with Amy over two years ago."

"I'm not talking about her. I'm talking about Gail. You know we weren't even friendly before all this."

"Are you so sure that you couldn't have been?" Wan grinned. "What do they say about fighting like cats and dogs, and what it means about channeling energy?"

"Whoa, slow down there. You're jumping the gun."

"I'm not so sure about that."

Lily hit her leg with her fist. "I'm not sure I'm ready for it."

"That's fine. You can be not ready. I'm sure Gail would want you to take all the time you need. Just talk to her. She doesn't deserve to be treated poorly."

"All right. I'll call her when I get home."

"Thank you." Wan maneuvered the car off the interstate and along the surface streets. When they were stopped by a red light, he murmured, "Someday, and I'm not saying when, you'll thank me for insisting you do this."

"You want to say I told you so, don't you?"

"Yep."

"Okay. I'll keep that in mind." Lily stopped talking, taking in the sight of her neighborhood, and finally, her house.

She had used bonuses from work to put a down payment on a small place in Noe Valley. The garage was at street level. Even contemplating the steps up to the main entrance, or the thought of the stairs to her bedroom on the top floor, could not stop the burst of pleasure she felt.

"Man," she whispered. "It is so good to be home."

CHAPTER FIFTEEN

Lily stayed polite, but she was very happy to watch the taillights of Wan's car speeding away from the vantage point of her living room window. For a few minutes after she locked the door, she leaned against it and listened.

There was a particular sound to the silence in her house. Faintly, she heard the noise from the freeway, a ticking as the outside siding expanded in the afternoon sun, and a hum from the refrigerator. She pushed the walker in front of her, smiling at the familiar creaking of a floorboard near the kitchen.

Lily wandered around her house, moving slowly because she had to push the walker ahead of her. She had to stop many times to find a way around obstructions. After all the time she spent homeless, she had become a pack rat and had managed to fit a lot of furniture into the small space. It was a very eclectic look since she had found most of the furnishings and things on the sidewalk after other people discarded them.

She touched the knickknacks and smiled at the memories they evoked. She also noticed little signs that her teammates had been around: cards on the mantel, little notes in the bathroom, and funny labels on all the ready-made meals in the refrigerator. Her heart lightened when she found each new message.

Sitting down in the den, she fingered the television remote. She had gotten her fill of daytime TV when she had spent so many hours on her stomach in the hospital. Setting the remote aside, she started to reach for the phone on the end table, but stopped when her already abused muscles gave a twinge.

Getting up, Lily took the phone, looked at the buttons, and realized she did not know Gail's number. She could call Wan, but she was tired of being teased by him. Instead, she went to the pile of papers at the top of one of the boxes that Wan had set by the front door.

Searching through all the materials from the hospital and the physical therapist, she finally found a sheet with Gail's phone number. She punched in six of the seven numbers before hanging up the phone. What would she say if Gail answered the call?

There had to be a good way to let Gail know she had left another place without actually telling her. Lily paced, trying to figure out the best way to tell Gail that she was home. The more she thought about it, the more she realized that Gail had every right to be upset over not being told earlier.

Stomping her foot, Lily decided she would just go ahead and do it. She punched all seven digits into the phone and lifted the receiver to her ear.

The phone rang three times before Gail answered. "Hello?"

"Hey, Gail. It's me, Lily."

"Lily! How nice to hear from you. Is everything okay?"

"Yeah, things are great."

"Good. Are you calling from the payphone on the first floor? You don't sound out of breath at all."

"Um, no." Lily cleared her throat. "I'm...uh...calling from home."

"Home? Your home? In San Francisco?"

"Yeah. Wan just dropped me off."

"But I thought—"

Lily interrupted. "You are the first person I'm calling to let know."

"I'm glad you thought about me. I would have hated to drive down to San Mateo only to find out you'd been released."

Lily bit her lip and replied, "I know. It was wrong of me to do that the first time, and I didn't want to do something like that again."

"Glad to hear it. Was there any other reason why you called?"

"To tell you I was back at home, and maybe see if you and Sierra would like to bring Butch back tonight."

"I would be happy to bring your dog over to you," Gail said in a clipped tone.

"What's wrong?"

"Nothing."

"No, there is. I can't tell much, but I can tell that." Lily sighed. "I don't just want my dog, you know. I want to see you and Sierra. I've got plenty of food. You're welcome to come for dinner."

"Really?" Gail sounded much warmer.

"Really. I miss it when I don't see you guys."

"Thank you. That almost makes up for you not asking me to come and get you."

"Will it help if I tell you I should have?" Lily found that telling Gail was easier than she'd imagined.

"It does help to hear that."

Trying to lighten things up, Lily said, "Yeah, Wan's car was almost too small to carry all the stuff I managed to collect while I was in rehab, and he drives like a maniac."

"You should have stopped while you were ahead."

"I'm sorry I didn't tell you beforehand."

"I thought we had covered this after the last disappearing incident."

"I'm not that fast a learner."

"That is becoming clearer by the minute."

"Hey! I just got home. You shouldn't be abusing me already."

"You haven't seen abuse yet." Gail cleared her throat. "Do you understand why I'm upset?"

"I think so."

"So why did you do something that would upset me?"

"Because I'm an idiot?"

"Seriously, Lily!"

Easing down onto the couch, Lily tried to explain herself. "I keep forgetting that you're different. I'm not used to taking somebody else under consideration for my every move."

"I'm not asking you to do that. Just to know that I want to be there for you." Gail sighed. "Look, it is really hard to have this sort of conversation over the phone. Why don't we try to talk more when Sierra, Butch and I come by?"

"You'll come?"

"I'd be stupid to turn down an opportunity to see your crib."

"Great. See you around five o'clock?"

"Sierra has practice, so it will be closer to six o'clock. Is that too late?"

"No. I'm going to take a nap."

"You're not going to run around cleaning, are you?"

"I don't need to," Lily answered smugly. "My team cleaned the whole place after they fixed it up."

"You'll have to show me all they did."

"I'll give you the nickel tour."

"Excellent. Is there anything we can bring?"

"Um, only if you want to drink something other than water or soda."

"No, that's fine. We'll see you soon."

"I'm looking forward to it. Bye." Lily hung up the phone and carried it with her to the kitchen. She caught a glimpse of her grinning face in the reflection of a stainless steel saucepan. She touched her lips, wondering if she always smiled this much when she talked to Gail.

She realized she was really looking forward to seeing Gail and Sierra. Getting to know both of them had been the best thing to come out of the accident and its aftermath. Not that she wanted to go through that agony again just to gain a friend, she said to herself.

Remembering just how much energy Sierra had and adding in her dog's exuberance, Lily headed upstairs. A nap now was the only way she would be coherent for her and Gail to talk later.

Stairs were still difficult with the walker, so she left it at the base of the stairs and relied entirely on her new cane. She thought she might have to go out and get one with a sword inside once she had healed up a little more. Highly illegal, she knew, but the thought of having one made the thought of needing a cane much more palatable.

She took half a pain pill and eased her way into the bed. She had found the best way to sleep was either on her stomach or on her back with her knees raised. In any other position, her back would stay tense and she would be jarred from sleep when her muscles cramped.

Just a short time later, Lily turned off the alarm and dragged herself into the bathroom to splash her face with water. Taking a moment to admire the bars around the tub and toilet, she had to admit she was actually pretty impressed with the work her teammates had done.

After returning downstairs, Lily went through the refrigerator until she found a casserole that did not look entirely vegetable based. She did not mind healthy food, but she didn't know if Sierra might be a typical teenager who hated to eat veggies.

She put the casserole in a low oven and went to the front room to wait for her guests. As she sat there, she played with one of Butch's squeaky toys, thinking about how much she missed her beast. Suddenly, she heard the sound of Gail's car, and then a deep bark from her dog.

Lily grinned until her face ached when she opened the door. Butch was so excited that she jumped, squirmed and danced into the house.

Smiling a welcome at Sierra and Gail, Lily led the way to the living room where she eased herself onto the floor and let Butch climb on top of her to get a good rubbing. Finally, Butch calmed down and she pulled herself up.

"Welcome to my home," she said to Gail and Sierra.

"Thank you." Gail smirked, "I think you can take it that Butch missed you."

"We have never spent that much time apart since I got her," Lily admitted.

"Now that you're home, you'll be wanting her back, won't you?" Gail asked.

"Well, it might not be a good idea to try and handle her full time." Lily looked at Sierra. "Butch looks like she's been really well cared for. Thank you so much."

"I fed her, and took her for walks, and played with her every night," Sierra said.

"And let her sleep with you at night," Gail put in.

"Oh, she didn't need any more spoiling. Anyway, I know I'm not up to walking her or doing all the things she needs. Would you be available to help me out?" Lily asked Sierra.

"I'd love to."

"Make sure your mom is okay with this, too."

"Mom can speak for herself," Gail said. "She's fine. How do you want to work this?"

"I can let Butch out in the backyard in the morning and at night, but she needs some exercise. Maybe coming over after school or practice for a long walk or something."

"We can do that."

"I can pay."

"That's okay," Sierra said. "Mom says I shouldn't expect payment for doing what I would want to do anyway."

"Not just money, but in dinner," Lily said. "I mean, I'd like both of you to come over as often as you can."

"Only if I can bring dinner over with us sometimes."

"I won't fight you on that. I've got a lot of missed and miserable meals to make up for." Lily blushed. "Do you want a tour? I'm afraid it will have to be a self-guided one as I don't want to climb the stairs again for a while."

"No problem. We can wander."

When Gail and Sierra returned to the main room a short time later, Lily pulled the casserole out of the oven. "Ready for dinner?"

"Oh, yeah," answered Sierra.

"Sure. What are we having?" Gail asked.

"This is one of the dinners my team left for me. I've got enough food for an army now."

"That's a good thing, right? It will save you having to cook."

"But I miss cooking." Lily grinned. "Sierra, tell me about practice."

As the girl began chatting on about her team and her afternoon, Lily leaned back in her chair. The homey scene was just what she needed on her first night out of rehab.

The meal went by pretty fast, the conversation flowing easily between her and her guests. Lily's stomach was sore from laughing once the dishes were clean, and Gail and Sierra were ready to leave.

"I'll see you tomorrow?" she asked Sierra, after she hugged her goodbye.

"Yes. We'll be here at about the same time," Sierra answered.

"Good." Lily looked at Gail. "I'm sorry we didn't get to talk. I mean about other stuff."

"Even though we didn't, I feel better after dinner and everything."

"Yeah. Me, too."

"Good. Maybe tomorrow we'll get to probe your psyche in depth."

Lily pretended to shudder. "No, no. Anything but that."

Leaning forward quickly, Gail placed a kiss on Lily's cheek, earning a raised eyebrow. "Well, if my daughter gets a hug, I get a kiss."

"More like steal a kiss," Lily said. She touched her cheek and felt a flutter of pleasure in her chest.

Gail waved her hand. "Semantics. Have a good evening. Call me if you need anything."

"I will. Thank you."

Closing the door, Lily watched the two Joiner women get into the car and drive away. She looked down into Butch's warm brown eyes. "It is just you and me, sport."

Butch barked and happily followed Lily, but pushed by when she took too long to climb the stairs. By the time Lily stepped into the bedroom, the dog had ensconced herself on the bed.

"Looks like you've been spoiled lately," Lily said. "If I hadn't missed you so badly, there is no way I'd let you stay up here tonight."

Butch made a smug sounding bark.

"Okay. For tonight only." Lily eased herself onto the bed and petted the soft muzzle Butch pushed under her hand.

She fell asleep safe in the knowledge that she was exactly where she wanted to be.

CHAPTER SIXTEEN

Three days later, that good night of sleep was just a memory. She had been reducing the pain medication and was finding it harder to fall asleep without the pills. It had not been pain, though, that kept her awake all night. The late night phone call from Ken Williams really bothered her. She had spent hours afterward, tossing in bed and trying to work out what to do.

She remembered being happy when the telephone rang, thinking it was Gail. On the evenings when she and Sierra didn't stay for dinner, Gail would always call to wish her goodnight. Their conversations would go on for a while, neither of them willing to hang up.

Ken's call was a different matter. She had been surprised to hear from him, and was borderline rude since she wanted to clear the line for Gail to reach her.

"I'm going to cut to the chase," he had told her. "The company is in trouble, and I'm not even sure you can fix things."

"What are you talking about, Ken?"

"I'm talking about the production numbers. If you don't get them back in line with last year's by month's end, there are going to be a whole lot of people out of work."

Lily was confident that Wan had everything under control. "It can't be that bad," she had insisted.

"If all of the workers get laid off, I'm going to make sure you're out of a job with them."

She had laughed. "And how are you going to manage that?"

"Do you know how many OSHA regulations you violated by having a minor in the warehouse during work hours? I'm sure the kid's mother could point you to the relevant passages in the employee safety manual, and I'll be happy to tell worker's comp about the policy violations. You'd be lucky if they don't sue you to recover some of the money you've cost them."

She felt ill at the thought of losing her job and paying her medical bills, but the implied threat against Gail kept her awake. She didn't want to do anything that would hurt the company or Gail, but she needed to talk to Wan before she made any decisions.

Lily had been cleared to return to work but had not been cleared for driving, so she had a taxi pick her up and take her downtown. She had the paperwork from the hospital that qualified her for paratransit for the next few months. Signing up for that had to be done in person.

When she finished that chore, she headed to Tisane. She wanted to see the damaged warehouse for herself, talk to Wan and get in a few hours of work.

She slowly walked from the Embarcadero station to the Tisane corporate offices. Before going into the main building, she went around to the pier to look at the devastation from the outside, amazed to find the warehouse nearly completely rebuilt. All the rubble was gone, as was the ship.

"Different, huh?" a man said from behind her.

"Sorry, what?" asked Lily as she turned. She smiled to see one of the dockworkers. "Ramon! Good to see you."

"*Sí*, it is good to know you're on your feet again."

"You're telling me." She shrugged. "I expected the warehouse to look worse."

"It was very bad for many days. The ship that overturned, it was good when that one was finally taken away."

"I bet it was. It almost doesn't seem real to me, you know?"

"Not real? You were in there!"

"I know, but I wasn't in any condition to see much of anything once it happened."

"There are pictures."

"Oh?"

"*Sí*. The lawyers took many pictures and the television crews took video."

Lily grimaced. "I'm not sure I want to see a playback of me being pulled from the wreckage. I guess I should go see what the inside is like." She moved slowly to the entrance, and was shocked at how empty it seemed.

"Hey, boss," said another familiar voice.

"Darrell! Good to see you, buddy." Lily was genuinely happy to see the dock supervisor. He had made a couple of trips to the rehab center to see her during her recovery and had kept her apprised of things at work.

"I'm really glad to see you back on your feet."

"Me, too." Lily waved her hand. "What's up with all the space?"

"What wasn't contaminated by the collapse was moved out by hand and sold in bulk. There was no place to store it while we were getting the building back up."

"And we haven't had time to restock the inventory?"

"We only got the occupational permit last week and have started to ramp up the incoming, but we've got so many back orders that most everything is going right back out again. It's also been hard to get some of the stuff we lost."

"Yeah, tea plants only grow so fast. Let me look at the purchase orders and see if I can speed some things along."

"Great. It is so good to hand it over to you."

"Thanks, I think." Lily followed him to her rebuilt office, her eyes widening at the pile of papers covering the desk.

"Oh, about that," Darrell said. "We didn't know if you were using the same filing system, so we've been leaving everything out."

"Wonderful." Lily put her hand on the nearly foot high stack. "I guess I need to start by getting this stuff put away."

"Just tell a couple of the guys how to do it and we'll get it done for you. I've had to send some of our people home because there isn't enough work."

Lily nodded. "All right. Send them in and I'll give them something to do."

Two hours later, most of the filing cabinets had been put in order and relabeled. The dockworkers finally started putting paper in the hanging files.

Lily's back had really started to ache. "Okay, guys, keep plugging away. I'm going to go check in the main office before I call it a day."

"No problem, boss," Darrell answered.

"I know. That's why I feel okay about leaving."

Lily slowly walked back to the main building. Since the pain made it hard to move quickly, she found herself constantly stopped by her co-workers, most of whom seemed happy to see her. Finally, she made it to the corner office on the top floor.

"Hey, Carla. Is the boss in?" she asked Wan's secretary.

"Oh, you're a sight for sore eyes." Carla jumped up and came around the desk with her arms stretched out.

"Gently," Lily reminded her.

"Of course." Carla smiled and gave her a hug. "I'm so glad to see you."

"Really?"

"Yes, with you gone there was no one here who could keep him in line."

Lily winked. "Considering all the time he spent with me, I'm surprised that was a problem."

"Oh, it's that new VP. He's been such a pain in the back end." Carla lowered her voice. "I think he's trying to oust Mr. Yanhai."

Lily was really starting to dislike Ken Williams. Before last night's call, she had found his smarmy manner annoying. If he was gunning for Wan, that made him dangerous. "That's not going to happen. Wan can handle anything that jerk can dish out."

"Now that you're back he can."

"You give me too much credit. I'm just one woman."

The phone started ringing, so Carla returned to her desk to answer the call. She said before picking up the receiver, "But you're the glue and he'll be so glad to see you. Go right in." Into the phone, she said, "Hello, Wan Yanhai's office."

Lily pushed open the heavy oak door and stepped into the large room. She saw Wan leaning close to his monitor and said, "You're going to go blind."

He whirled around, grinning. "Hey. I didn't expect you in so soon."

"I wanted to get any paperwork moving so I can start working for a living again."

"You aren't pushing yourself too hard, are you?"

"No, Dad. I'm taking it easy."

Wan nodded approvingly. "You're looking well. Standing up suits you."

She waggled the cane. "I'm not sure that I'd be doing so good if it weren't for this. So tell me, what has Carla's panties in a twist?"

"It's nothing." Wan glanced at his desk and moved papers from one pile to another.

"Really? Then what are you hiding under there?"

"Oh, that's just a little thing. There is nothing to worry about."

"Really? That isn't what I heard."

"Oh?"

"Or what I saw. The warehouse is nearly empty."

"I can handle it."

Lily wasn't convinced, but she turned toward the door. "Why don't you come over to my place tonight and we'll talk?"

"I can't. I'll be working late."

Now she knew something was wrong. Lily turned around. "Working late?" she echoed.

"Yes, the board wants some reports before the end of the week."

"Since when do they start demanding things outside of the quarterly meetings?"

"They've got new committees meeting monthly."

Lily cocked her head. "Seriously, dude. What's up?"

"They seem to think my laissez-faire management style is responsible for the recent downturn in sales, and might even have contributed to the loss of the warehouse."

"How's that, exactly? You were supposed to be out at the end of the dock using your superpowers to shield us from an out-of-control container ship?"

"If we had moved most of the operations down to Hayward as proposed, we wouldn't have been paying high rents, and we certainly would not have been in a place where a boat could nearly wipe out our operations so that, a month later, we're only just now getting back to normal." Wan shook his head. "It doesn't look good."

"Does it matter what they think? I mean, it's your company."

"Not anymore. I made a lot of sacrifices to break Republic's monopoly on the Midwest. The result of all those deals means I'm no longer the majority stockholder."

"I didn't know that." Lily sat down in the chair in front of his desk. "Can't you explain things to them?"

"We're a little beyond that."

"Since when? I thought you and the board got along."

"I do get along with the board as a whole. Lately, though, there's been a push for these committees to have more oversight, and things have become more acrimonious. In the last couple of months, there have also been a lot more outsiders called in as experts. They've been questioning every decision and every move we've made or were thinking of making even before the accident."

"That's strange, isn't it?"

"You bet. I'm trying to figure out who's behind it, but I've been so consumed with the new launch and the recovery that I haven't had a chance to work out what could be behind it all."

Lily attempted to lean forward and stopped with a small hiss of pain. "What can I do?"

"Get healthy and get the distribution numbers back up."

"That's what Ken said."

"What? When did you talk to him?"

"He called me at home yesterday."

"What exactly did he say?"

"He implied that I needed to take charge and get things cleared up by week's end, or it wouldn't just be me out of a job."

Wan scowled. "Things aren't that bad yet."

"But it doesn't sound good."

"Yes, it is true we're still dealing with fallout from the accident. Numbers are down across the board and everyone is going to have to do some belt tightening. We've got the cash reserves to weather the worst of it, but if we don't get raw material in and packaged tea out, we could lose our niche. Nobody will want to stock our stuff if we can't be relied on to restock as necessary."

"Don't they understand special circumstances?"

"Not in today's economy."

"That's harsh." Lily stood. "I'll go turn in my paperwork to Human Resources, but I'm here for you. The company is important to me, but you and my people mean even more."

"Thanks. Let me know what Gail says."

Lily hesitated at the door. "Um, Wan?"

"Yeah?"

"You know Gail and I have been…um…getting closer."

"About time!"

"Hey!" Lily frowned at his teasing. "I'm just checking if our dating would be a problem."

"We don't have a dating policy here, and besides, the two of you are in two separate departments. I don't think it will be an issue."

"Even though we're both directors? Even in the current environment?"

"I think you should follow your heart. If the board has a problem, we'll deal with it together."

"Not that there is anything to deal with, you know. I'm just checking."

"I appreciate that you did, but love is more important than work."

"That's just because you have savings to fall back on when work isn't there."

"No, it is because I have someone I love to fall back on when all else goes wrong." Wan shook his head. "Love is worth fighting for, Lily."

Lily bit her tongue against an immediate denial. What she was building with Gail and Sierra was different from her past experiences with those who professed to love her.

Whatever it was called, she knew she'd fight to keep it.

CHAPTER SEVENTEEN

Gail stood in the doorway of her office talking to Chet when she saw Lily approach. Before Lily reached the Human Resources department, Ken Williams stepped into the hall.

"Ah, Lily. So good to see you up and about."

"You are too, too kind," she answered.

Slapping her on the back, Ken laughed heartily. "You're such a card."

Gail's jaw dropped. She would not have believed her eyes if she had not seen the insensitive jerk strike Lily herself. She felt a rush of anger when Lily paled from the pain.

Coming out of her office, she took hold of Lily's arm. "There you are. You're late for our meeting," she said, leading her inside and closing the door. Once they were away from Ken, she asked, "My goodness, are you okay?"

"Just give me a minute to get my breath back."

"Has he always treated you that way?"

"Since I walked in on him at the holiday party with someone not his wife."

"You could destroy his marriage."

"I wouldn't."

"I know that now." Gail dragged her toward the couch. "People ascribe to others their own motives. He expects you to blackmail him, and because you haven't, he figures you're tormenting him." She pointed downward. "Sit down."

"Why?"

"You've got to be in pain. How long have you been standing today?"

"A few hours."

"And how many is a few?"

"Five or so."

"You are supposed to take breaks to sit or lie down every hour, aren't you?" She waited for a nod. "Have you taken a break all day?"

"No. There hasn't been an opportunity."

"Make it then. You can't afford to relapse."

Lily muttered, "You can say that again."

"What?"

"Nothing."

Gail stared at Lily for a moment before sighing. "I know I sort of kidnapped you when I saw what Ken did. Were you actually at this end of the building to see me?"

"Yeah. Have you got a minute or two for us to meet?"

"Sure." Gail sat down in her chair. "You still look a bit pale."

"My back's just twinging a little."

"Is that Lily-speak for you're going insane with pain?"

Lily grinned. "It is not quite that bad."

"Good." Gail could not help smiling back. "I've gotten the letter from your doctor clearing you to work a limited schedule for the next couple of weeks."

"Yeah, I'm ready to work."

"Really? Are you sure you're up to working full days?"

"I can do it."

"Be honest, Lily. Do you need to ease back into things?"

"I want to do my job." She clenched her fists. "I need to do my job."

"I know. I just don't want you to overextend yourself."

"There is just so much that needs to be done."

"There always is."

"No, this is different."

"Tell me."

"Ken called me yesterday. He says I need to get the production numbers up to pre-accident status by month end."

"That's two weeks."

"I know."

"That is an unreasonable demand." Furious, Gail ticked off the points on her fingers, "The warehouse was in shambles. The dock was unsafe. You were injured."

"Yeah, about that."

"What?"

"He says it wasn't in the performance of my job duties."

"What are you talking about? You were in the warehouse. At work."

Lily shrugged.

"Talk to me. What can he possibly..." Gail furrowed her brow. "What's going on?"

"What do you mean?"

"I know you. Normally you'd be beating back challengers to your domain tooth and nail."

"So?"

"What's stopping you?" She studied Lily, noting the downturned gaze.

"It isn't anything I can't handle. Besides, it won't even matter if I get the numbers back up."

Gail studied Lily. "You're a fighter. If you're not fighting, it is because you're protecting someone else. Who is he using against you?"

Lily sighed. "He tells me he is going to ask for worker's comp to review my case."

"On what grounds?"

"That having a minor in the warehouse is a direct violation of any number of safety policies."

"That son of a bitch. I can't believe he'd use my daughter. Or threaten me."

"Don't worry. I won't let anything happen to either of you."

"Nothing is going to happen to anyone." Gail replied. "The rules apply to work days and child labor, not holidays and visitors. I doubt that anyone with any sense would want to take on the bad publicity they'd garner by going after a local hero."

"Stop calling me that."

"If you do something as foolish as caving into Ken's bullying, I will!" Gail could not believe Lily wasn't angrier. "What does Wan have to say about this?"

"I didn't tell him every detail of my conversation. He's got his own problems with the board giving him a hard time."

"I've had visits from several efficiency experts myself, but I thought he had approved of what they were doing."

"He says that his hand has been forced."

"Since the accident?"

"No, longer. It started after those clashes with Republic." Lily thought for a moment. "That was right around when Ken was hired, too. Since then, we've been going from one crisis to another."

"You think Ken is to blame for the ship captain's stroke?"

"No, but you've got to admit it looks suspicious." Lily gusted out a breath of air. "It doesn't help his case that I don't appreciate him calling me at home. He basically threatened me. Vice president or not, he doesn't have the right."

Gail nodded approvingly at the passion in Lily's voice. "So what are you going to do?"

"I know my department and the distribution channels for tea better than anyone. With the warehouse and dock operational, we can kick things into high gear."

"Sounds good, but you know that you're not alone, right? You've got good people working for you, don't you?"

"Of course."

"Then have them take on some of the heavy lifting. You focus on what you can do from a desk and delegate the rest."

"I'm not used to leading from behind."

"I know it isn't your style, but we aren't talking about forever. It will just be until you're back to one hundred percent." Gail smiled. "You've come a long way from the woman whose heart stopped. Give your body a break and let it heal a bit before you start scaling any mountains."

"I'm not talking about Everest. I'm talking about doing what I need to do to get the tea flowing and the business back in the black."

"Right now you have to consider molehills as mountains. Husband your energy and you'll make progress. Squander it quickly and you could relapse."

Lily sighed and rubbed her temples. "Taking it slow is hard for me."

Coming around her desk, Gail slid in to the chair next to Lily. "I am starting to understand that. You know I am here for you. For support, for friendship, maybe even a little more someday."

Lily looked at her. "I know, and I'm starting to realize that I need you." She swallowed. "For your support, and your friendship, and maybe even something more."

"Truly?"

"Yeah." Lily wiped her brow. "I...uh...asked Wan about it."

"You did?" Gail's voice broke. She flushed. "What exactly did you ask him?"

"If there would be any problems." Lily dropped her gaze. "You know, if there were work issues that would get in the way."

"I'm the director of human resources, couldn't you have asked me?"

"Um, what?"

"You had to ask the company president? My boss?" Gail pinched the bridge of her nose. "Can I just ask why you felt compelled to tell him?"

"He's not just my boss. He's my best friend."

Gail struggled to find calm. "All right. I understand that. Telling friends is important."

"I also didn't want him to be blindsided by it if it was a problem."

"I respect that."

"I thought he should know."

"Before me?" Gail raised her hand and lowered her voice. "Sorry, forget I said that."

"Was I wrong?"

"Not at all. His opinion is important to you."

"And I wanted him to tell me this was the right thing to do."

"Did he?"

"He said love was worth fighting for."

Gail jerked a little in surprise at Lily using that word. "We haven't even gone on a date yet."

"Well, haven't you thought about it? I mean, we've had dinner together nearly every night and we get along so well. All of us."

"Sierra adores you."

"She's great and I want to be a part of you guys' lives."

"You already are." Gail stared into Lily's dark eyes. "You and Butch are family."

"When my parents kicked me out, I hated the idea of family. You and Sierra have changed my mind and opened my heart." After a pause, Lily asked, "Are you really mad about me talking to Wan?"

"No, sweetheart. He is important to you and that makes him important to me. As much as I might regret my personal and work lives colliding, I will never, for a single minute, be anything but grateful that you are a part of both."

Lily blushed. "I think that's the nicest thing anyone has ever said to me."

"Well, it won't be the last. I tend to get a little gooey when I open my heart. Just ask Sierra." Gail laughed. "She claims she'll be diabetic if I don't stop."

"I can imagine worse ways to go," Lily said, grinning.

"I'll keep that in mind."

"So we're good?"

"Yeah. We are."

Standing up, Lily prepared to leave. "Will you be stopping by later?"

"Oh, yeah. That reminds me. Sierra is being dropped off by one of the moms from her soccer team. I've got a meeting with one of the committees. I should have asked you first but..."

"It isn't a problem. I'm glad you trust her with me."

"I do." Gail sank back down into her chair. "Now you go home and rest so you have the energy to deal with her when she arrives."

"Yes, ma'am," Lily replied as she walked through the door.

"Hey, Chet? Did you hear that? That's the proper way to respond to my commands."

Chet and Lily simultaneously rolled their eyes, and then burst out laughing.

CHAPTER EIGHTEEN

For a while after Lily left, Gail stared sightlessly at her monitor. She was now out in a big way with her boss and, despite her discomfort, she could not stop the smile that the thought of getting closer to Lily brought to her face.

The smile faded as she contemplated what Lily had told her about Ken and the company finances. Raising her voice, she called, "Chet?"

"You bellowed?"

"Yeah. Have you heard anything about the board giving Wan a hard time?"

"Carla mentioned something about him working late. Maybe he's been spending too much time at the hospital."

"Any idea what he's working on?"

"No. If you want, I can use the assistant's grapevine to find out."

"Please do, but be subtle. I wouldn't want to overplay our hand."

"I can do subtle." Chet blushed at Gail's raised eyebrow and full body scan. He currently wore a lilac suit with a yellow polka-dot shirt. "This is just protective camouflage. Trust me, they'll never see me coming."

"I hope so. Thanks." Gail drummed her fingers on the desk. She was confident that Chet would try his best, but she feared ferreting out what was really going on would take more than water cooler gossip.

She smiled suddenly when she remembered someone who might help. Her ex-husband's younger brother now worked as a security consultant, but he had started out as a hacker. Jason was a bit of a privacy nut, so she knew not to try calling him from her cell phone.

"I'm going to take a walk to clear my head. Tell anyone who calls I'll be back in a few," she told Chet as she walked out of the office.

Gail took a left out of the building and strolled down to the Ferry Building. Dropping change into the first pay phone she came across, she dialed a number she had memorized more than a decade ago. She heard several rings and clicks, and more ringing as the call was routed across the world, for all she knew.

Jason abruptly answered the call. "How clean is your phone?"

"It's a pay phone," Gail said.

"Go ahead, then."

"It's Gail. Gail Joiner." During a long pause, she heard tapping on a keyboard.

"Not Gail, my ex-sister in law?" he asked.

"The one and only."

"Long time, no hear. Do you remember the first birthday present I gave your daughter?"

"You mean the Furby you modified to swear and tell completely inappropriate jokes? The one that gave her nightmares?"

"She was only a couple years old. I didn't traumatize her for life."

"I was! The first time I heard it over the baby monitor saying it was hungry for brains, I nearly had a heart attack!"

"Yeah, that was fun. Except for sewing the fur back on. That was a pain."

"You're a menace to society."

"Aw, you say the sweetest things. I assume, though, you have a reason for the call."

Gail swallowed. "I have a favor to ask. There is something weird going on at my job."

"Tell me more."

"It's a lot of little things not adding up. The board is strangely active and interfering. I need to know if I'm becoming a crazy conspiracy theorist like you, or if there really is an effort to destroy the company."

"Bottom line?"

"If true, I could use some shark repellent."

"As long as it doesn't involve overthrowing the government, I can do it. Regime change would revoke my security clearance." He paused. "Any ideas who is behind things?"

"I know who I want it to be."

"Who?"

"Ken Williams, the vice president of marketing."

"Why?"

"You know about what happened on the pier? The accident?"

"Sure, I saw the coverage. I'm glad the kid is okay."

"Thanks. Ken is trying to use Sierra as leverage against the woman who was hurt."

"Can he do that?"

"His accusations could trigger an audit by our worker's compensation carrier. It is highly unlikely the carrier will actually cancel the coverage, but it is stress she doesn't need." Gail looked over her shoulder. "There may be more to it. If Ken uses Sierra to make a liability issues case, I'll be put in the crosshairs too."

"That's no good, but is there a connection?"

"I'm honestly not sure. I do know that before the accident, Lily and I weren't friendly, and I had no complaints from the board. We've been getting closer, though, and I've suddenly got piles of metrics and benchmarking reports now due."

"I will look into it and see what I find. If he is trying to come after you and Sierra, do you mind if I manage some mischief?"

"Not at all. He's a prick and deserves it." Gail unfolded a piece of paper. "I've got a list of the current board members too. Can you see if anyone is getting leaned on or is masterminding things?"

"Read it out."

Gail read out the list, spelling a number of the last names. "Thanks, Jason," she said when she finished.

"I'll do my best to get you some answers. I should have some preliminary information in the next two days." Without another word, he disconnected the call.

Feeling a little lighter for having started the investigation, Gail returned to her office and focused on her work. Her recent assignment from the board's personnel committee centered on a tedious collection of metrics on turnover and retention. Now that she was thinking about it, she wondered about the ulterior motives for the work. While the normal course of events could include the board's governance responsibilities requesting direct reports from department heads, the fact they had never done so before made the timing a bit suspicious.

She spent the afternoon pulling up raw data and putting it in a detailed report. When she finally e-mailed a copy to the committee, she wondered if any of it would be used against the current management team. After sending a second copy to Wan with a summary of what she had told the committee, she shut down her computer.

Out in the parking lot, Gail sent a text to Lily before getting in her car. She wanted to know if she should bring food when she swung by to pick up Sierra. Not getting a reply and deciding it was better to be safe than sorry, she stopped off for fast food. Burgers and fries might not be what the doctor ordered, but they sure would hit the spot.

Juggling the bags when she got out of the car at Lily's house, Gail couldn't help basking in the warm feelings that coming home to Lily gave her. She was eagerly welcomed by Sierra, Lily and Butch, and quickly tugged up the stairs to the table for dinner.

After the second time Sierra nearly shot milk out of her nose from laughing, Gail held up her hand. "Okay, enough frivolity. We've got to all calm things down a bit or we're going to all have upset stomachs tonight."

Lily and Sierra simultaneously whined, "Aw, Mom."

Raising a single eyebrow, Gail glared at the two miscreants.

"Uh-oh," Sierra whispered.

"What?" Lily asked.

"That's Mom's not fooling around anymore look."

"The weird eyebrow thing?"

"Yeah, disobey that on pain of a spanking."

Lily blushed and choked on a mouthful of french fries. "Seriously?"

"Darn right," Gail answered. "You wouldn't want to earn a spanking, would you?" When Lily coughed some more, she winked at her. "Don't worry, I'd go easy on you the first time."

Scrubbing a hand over her face to wipe away the blush, Lily seemed too tongue-tied to formulate an answer.

Gail gathered up the food wrappers and crumpled them into the bag. "Sierra, take Butch for a walk around the block, and then we have to go."

"Do we have to?"

"Yes, I know you have more homework."

"Not that much more."

"Well, Lily had her first day back at work today. She needs to get some rest so she'll be ready to tackle a full day at work tomorrow."

Reminding her about Lily's injuries proved the magic phrase to end Sierra's complaining and get her moving. Clipping the leash to Butch's collar, she dashed outside and down the front stairs with the dog.

Gail closed the door and turned back to the dining room to find that Lily had come up behind her. "I hope she remembered to bring a plastic bag with her."

"She usually does." Lily lightly touched Gail's arm. "I had a really good time with her this afternoon."

"I'm glad you two are getting along so well. There have been very few women that I've wanted to bring into her life, and fewer still who wanted to be a part of ours."

"I do."

"Mmm, I like the way you say that. Is it too early to post the marriage banns? I mean we haven't even hired the U-Haul yet." Gail did not have to wait long for a flush to climb Lily's neck and stain her cheeks.

Lily stomped her foot. "Stop making me blush!"

"I have to say the color red suits you."

Lily laughed and stuck out her tongue.

In a move that surprised both of them, Gail lunged at her. She grabbed ahold of the collar of Lily's shirt and wrapped her lips around Lily's provocative tongue. When Lily pulled her tongue back in her mouth, Gail gently bit her bottom lip.

Holding still a centimeter from Lily's mouth, Gail asked, "As you can see, there are a lot of other things you could be doing with that tongue."

Lily hummed in anticipation. "Hmm, I thought we were going to take things slow."

"Slow or glacial?" Gail asked. Starting another kiss, she carefully walked Lily into the nearest wall, smiling at the way Lily's lips vibrated against hers when she moaned as her shoulders made contact with the wall's cool surface.

Gail loathed the idea of ever ending the kiss, but she was aware that Sierra could come back any minute. With infinite regret, she quickly pressed her lips once more against Lily's before reluctantly breaking the kiss.

"Don't stop," Lily panted.

The dilated pupils in Lily's eyes and the quiet plea nearly made Gail forget their location, and dive back into the taste and touch of Lily's lips. She brushed aside a teardrop hanging from Lily's lashes and stroked her soft cheek.

"I don't want to ever stop, but I don't think either of us is ready to explain to Sierra what we're doing."

"But we are doing this, right?"

Gail smiled tenderly. "Most definitely."

The click of canine toenails on the stairs grew louder. Gail let her hand fall to her side. "Sorry I started something I can't finish."

Lily coughed and muttered, "I'm sort of a fan of delayed gratification."

"Now that is good to know." Opening the door for Sierra and Butch to enter, Gail laughed softly. "You may regret telling me that."

"I thought you would only use your powers for good."

Leaning in close to pick up her purse, Gail whispered in Lily's ear, "When I'm good, I'm very good, but when I'm bad, I'm better." She said to Sierra more loudly, "Don't forget your homework."

"Yes, Mom," Sierra replied.

"Sweet dreams, Lily. Take it easy tomorrow and take plenty of breaks."

"Yes, Mom," Lily said mockingly.

Gail wagged her finger. "My intentions toward you are distinctly nonmotherly."

"Should it be yes, ma'am, then?"

The sound of those words and the way Lily dipped her head slightly when saying them tickled Gail deep inside. "That would be more appropriate. Now go to bed."

"Yes, ma'am."

Sierra headed out the door. "I don't even want to know."

Gail followed her daughter to the car, and for the longest moment, could not take her eyes off the closed front door of Lily's house. Her body still thrummed from the kiss.

"You like her."

"Yeah," Gail answered. Turning to Sierra, she asked, "That's not going to be a problem is it?"

"No, she's cool."

"And I'm not?"

"She definitely raises your stats."

"Brat!" Gail growled before putting the car in reverse and backing out of the driveway. "Do you want to talk about it?"

"Eww!"

"Not details. Just about…stuff."

"This isn't your first girlfriend."

"No, but this is the first one you've known before we got together."

Sierra shrugged. "I'm okay." She put her feet up on the dash. "And your seeing her means I get to still take care of Butch."

Accelerating through a yellow light, Gail shook her head. "Great. Now I know I rank below the dog in the grand scheme of things."

"Aw, Mom. Don't be a drama llama."

"Excuse me?"

"You know, don't make a fuss about nothing."

"But why a llama?"

"Because a drama llama throws drama around like a llama spits. Everywhere!"

"I see."

Sierra fiddled with her shoelaces. "We both know you're a good mom."

"Thanks, sweetie. It is good to hear it sometimes, too." Gail downshifted to coax the car up San Francisco's hills. "You're a pretty darn good kid."

"Thanks. Does that mean I get a raise in my allowance?" At Gail's sideways glare, Sierra lifted both hands. "You can't blame me for asking while you're all mellow from making out."

"We were hardly making out."

"Whatever."

"Sierra, if you have questions about what you've seen or heard…" Gail paused. "Just wait a couple of years before asking, okay?"

"No worries, Mom. There are some things I just don't want to know."

Gail wiped her forehead. "Good. Now tell me about this test you nearly blew."

CHAPTER NINETEEN

Lily's back ached as she stood at the warehouse entrance with her clipboard at her hip. If it were possible for everything to go wrong, this was the day for it to happen. Two shipments were late, and then three others all arrived at the same time. As two of the shipments came by eighteen-wheelers, traffic was snarled through the parking lot.

She had to deal with corporate types who wanted their parking spaces back, construction workers wanting to bring in a load of Sheetrock, dockworkers manning the crane, and even an inventory control specialist snooping around with permission from the board.

When her phone rang, she was tempted to ignore it in favor of the four very large men crowding her space and demanding her attention. She had never been good at screening her calls. Without glancing at the caller ID, she held up a finger and flipped open her phone.

"Hey, Tiger," said one of her soccer teammates.

"What's up, Cindy? Things are a little busy here."

"This will just take a moment."

"Okay."

"I want to know whether you think it is better to ask permission or forgiveness?"

"Excuse me?" Lily signed the form thrust at her and turned her back to the chaos on the dock, typical for a Monday morning. "Do we have to do this now?"

"Um…sort of."

"Okay, what was the question again?"

"Do you think it is better to ask for permission before you do something, or seek forgiveness after you've done it?"

"Well, personally, I'm all for getting forgiveness."

"Glad to hear it. Bye!"

"Not so fast, girlfriend. Why do you need to know?"

"Well, we're setting up a welcome home party for you."

"Why would I have a problem with that?" Lily was actually pleased that her teammates were throwing her a party. She hated having to tell them that she didn't think she'd be able to play with them for a while. Even though she was feeling stronger every day, she had been afraid that she was going to lose their close camaraderie. This was the first time she had spoken to any of them since she had talked to them over the weekend.

"Because we are doing it at your house."

"What?"

"Yeah, we were thinking about what was best for you."

"Uh-huh."

"Sure. This way, when you get tired, you're already home and can just go to bed."

"Let me get this straight: you're throwing a party for me at my house?"

"You got it."

"How are you doing it? I'm at work."

"Oh, I've got a key."

"I gave you that for emergency use only."

"I know. Consider this a party emergency."

"There is no such thing," Lily scoffed.

"There should be," Cindy said. "If not, that's where the forgiveness comes in."

Lily sighed. "You're doing this now?"

"I am sitting in your driveway as we talk."

"Who's coming?"

"The team and anyone else we could wrangle for a weeknight party."

"Anyone from work?"

"Yeah. We invited Wan and Gail."

"So she knows about the party?"

"Of course. We told her yesterday."

"That rat. I saw her last night and she never said a single word."

"Ooh, keeping secrets already."

"I can't believe you guys are ganging up on me."

"We can't help it. It is amazing you're finally seeing someone that we like."

"What? How do you guys even know we're seeing each other? We haven't done hardly anything. Heck, we haven't even been on a date yet."

"Hello? You could power a city from the wattage of your smile when you talk about her or her kid."

"Sierra."

"What?"

"The kid has a name and it is Sierra."

"Whoa, easy there, Tiger." Cindy laughed. "See, that's another sign. You're getting protective of her daughter."

"Is that bad?"

"Not if you like her mother, it isn't." Cindy lowered her voice. "You do like her, don't you?"

"Yeah, but this isn't anything like Amy."

"Thank goodness for that. Women like Amy aren't the ones you build your life around. They are just for butterfly interludes, and if we expect them to be anything more, it only leads to disappointment and heartache." Cindy softened her tone. "Trust me, babe. It wasn't in her nature to play at making house."

"But is it in mine?"

"Most definitely. Since I've known you, you've been searching for home."

"No, I haven't," Lily immediately retorted. She paused. "Have I really?"

"Yes. I think you might have found it with Gail."

"How do I know for sure?"

Cindy laughed. "I don't know. When you find out, clue in the rest of us."

"I'm serious!"

"So am I. There isn't one answer. There is only what works for you." Cindy paused. "When you're not around her, do you think of her?"

"Yes."

"Is she your first thought on waking up and before you fall asleep? Does your heart beat faster when you see her caller ID on your phone, or her user name on new mail in your inbox?"

Lily could not help a smile. "Yeah."

"Do you think about her all day when she isn't with you, and when she is, you think about how much you will miss her when she goes away?"

"Yeah."

"To my mind, it is love when you care for them more than you care for yourself, and you put their needs before your own."

"I do that."

"Good girl. There's your answer."

"Was that how you knew?"

"I knew when I figured out that I did not want to exist without Karen. She was my life."

"And now she's your wife."

"Yep."

Lily turned to look at the dock. "Okay. You go do what you were planning to do while I get back to work. Am I supposed to be surprised?"

"Naw. You should accept a ride from Gail when she offers, though."

"Will do." Lily slid her phone back into her pocket and grinned at the waiting workers. "All right. Who was first?"

The rest of the day sped by quickly. She was kept too busy to worry or fret about what her teammates might be doing to her house. When the day wound down, she parked herself in her office. She was really starting to look forward to the piles of paperwork since they gave her a chance to get off her feet.

"Hey."

Lily turned to see Gail standing nearby. "Hey, yourself."

"You want a lift home?"

Signing the last page with a flourish, Lily gathered everything up. She toyed with the idea of turning the offer down, but felt too giddy about her newfound awareness of Gail's importance in her life. "I don't know," she said. "Do I want to ride with a rat fink?"

"What did you say?"

"I believe Raticus Finkus is the proper term."

"Hey!"

"You knew what my teammates were planning and you didn't tell me. You sat across from me at dinner last night and not a single word crossed your lips."

"I promised them." Gail blushed. "If you remember, we were busy with other things crossing our lips."

"I remember someone who brought dinner before kissing me to distraction. Who knew you had ulterior motives?" Lily closed the interoffice envelope she had put some papers in. "I just have to drop this off, and then I'll be ready to go."

As they walked through the lobby after dropping off the mail, Gail asked, "Are you really upset I didn't tell you?"

"No. I understand. You were worried about getting accepted by my buddies. Telling me could wreck their potential approval of you."

"I was worried about it affecting us. I hope they recognize the sacrifice I made."

"Well, they recognize how important you are to me. Cindy told me they like you too."

"Excellent. I love it when a plan comes together."

"Plan?"

"Of getting them on my side."

"Oh, yeah, the plan is working." Lily eased into the passenger seat of Gail's car. "Thanks for the lift." She leaned her head on the headrest and closed her eyes.

"Do you have the energy to do this?"

"I've got to. They planned it all out." Lily yawned. "They're good guys."

"I know." Gail turned down the radio and turned up the heat.

Lily felt the warmth on her lower body and murmured, "Thank you." She had been outside on the dock most of the day and her feet felt like blocks of ice.

"Have you taken a pain pill lately?"

"Not since lunch."

"Why don't you go ahead and do so?"

"Maybe I'd rather drink," Lily said. She opened an eye and looked at Gail's profile.

"Really?"

"Not really. I just wanted to see what you would say."

"It is your life, sweetheart. I just don't like to see you suffering."

"I know. I'll take a pill when we get there. I just don't have any water with me."

"Good." Gail swiftly navigated the vehicle across town. The rush hour traffic appeared to be no match for her knowledge of city streets. In a surprisingly short time, the car pulled up to Lily's house where a crowd of people waited inside the garage.

"Ready?" Gail asked.

"As I'll ever be," answered Lily. She stepped out of the car and into the welcoming arms of her friends.

Turning around when she reached the stairs, she glanced back to find a throng gathered around Gail as well. It did her heart good to see her family of choice so accepting of such a significant person in her life.

***

After the last guest left, Gail wandered around the house looking for Lily. She finally found her leaning against the counter in the kitchen.

"How are you doing?" she asked.

Lily glanced up. She had been leaning against the counter, swirling red wine around in a stemmed glass. "I'm okay. Starting to fade though."

"I thought you weren't going to drink."

"I haven't had more than a couple of sips. It was easier, after a while, to keep holding the glass rather than constantly explain about the meds."

"I'll trade you, then." Gail lifted the glass from Lily's fingers and replaced it with a highball glass filled with fruit.

"What is this?"

"Some special melon balls. Cindy made them."

"Special like the watermelon spiked with vodka? At least the Shiraz is good for my heart."

"No. Special as in there is a bit of bacon in the ball."

"Bacon? That's the perfect food."

"Indeed. Cindy also mentioned she put a bacon and mushroom casserole in the oven before she left."

"Yeah, we should eat something soon." Lily attempted to straighten up and winced.

"I suppose you neglected to take any more pain medication," Gail grumbled.

"Don't like the way it makes me feel," Lily said with a shrug and a grimace.

Gail took hold of Lily's hand and pulled her into the living room. With firm but gentle pressure, she eased her down on the couch. "Dinner won't be ready for another twenty minutes or so, and in the meantime, you have some tension that needs attending to."

"What kind of tension are we talking about?" Lily asked, waggling her eyebrows.

When Gail settled behind her to place steady hands on her shoulders and began to knead, Lily's head fell forward.

"I was talking about how tight your shoulders are, smart-ass." Gail slowly let her fingertips walk along the line of muscles in Lily's upper back. Pressing a little harder, she sought out the knots. "Of course, sometimes tending to one source of tension helps the others."

"What?" Lily tried to turn around. She hissed, tensing briefly.

"Easy, babe. It's just me, making you feel good."

Gail's hand slid up Lily's neck into her hair, gripping and tugging. Lily allowed herself to be handled, her head tipping back against Gail's shoulder while Gail kissed the shell of her ear.

"Easy for you to say," Lily mumbled. "You didn't have a building fall on you."

"I know," Gail replied quietly. She sniffed against a sudden prickling of tears.

"Gail." Lily's fingers splayed across her thigh. "I'm fine."

"I saw it happen, Lily. Right in front of me." Gail sighed. She leaned forward to breathe in the sweet scent from the curve of Lily's neck. "For the longest time, I had no idea if you and Sierra were even alive."

"We're both fine. You know that."

"I know I've never been so scared in my entire life." Gail bit her lip. "I don't think I'd survive if something like that happened again."

"Don't worry. A crash like that happens only once every million years." Lily smirked, a lazy upturn at the corners of her mouth that disappeared when she swiveled her head to glance in Gail's direction, her dark hair falling in front of her eyes.

Gail stared back at her. She watched as Lily lifted a hand to cup her cheek, and sighed when the pad of Lily's thumb traced the swell of her lower lip. She inhaled the dark scent of wine when Lily replaced her thumb with her mouth. Her arms encircled Lily's waist, carefully avoiding the healing places.

"How long did you say we had?" Lily asked.

"Twenty minutes," Gail answered "Maybe fifteen, now."

Lily gave Gail another kiss and relaxed when Gail eased her back around. Gail loved the feel of Lily cradled against her breasts.

It was Gail's turn to smirk when Lily willingly surrendered control of the situation and let her open her belt while mouthing a series of wet kisses over the column of Lily's throat.

At the sound of the zipper lowering, Lily whispered, "Gail, I...I don't know if I can..."

"You can." Gail's touch was gentle as she slid her hand between Lily's strong thighs.

Lily arched up to meet her touch when Gail's hand slipped beneath the waistband of her panties. "Oh!"

"Let me in," Gail murmured, the tip of her index finger tracing slowly over Lily's clit, circling around. "Focus on my touch. Just this, Lily."

Lily closed her eyes, her breathing shaky. She inhaled and whimpered on her exhale.

Gail's middle finger slipped inside of her. She kissed Lily's jaw as she pushed two fingers inside. She nipped at Lily's ear, and her fingers set an easy thrusting rhythm.

Her entire body tensing, Lily gritted her teeth and ground down on Gail's hand.

"Let go," Gail ordered, her lips brushing against Lily's hairline.

Between one moment and the next, Lily climaxed. As she caught her breath, she relaxed. Rolling her head against Gail's upper chest, she murmured, "The pain is gone."

"Do you want me to go into all the ways in which having an orgasm can actually be beneficial for the healing process?" Gail asked, withdrawing her fingers and licking them clean.

"Really?"

"Yep. Endorphins have a chemical structure similar to morphine."

"Is that why I want to sleep?"

"Indeed. Just relax while I go check on dinner." Gail winked. "Afterward, we can talk about future explorations of the endorphin effect."

"That'll be fun."

"Which is why you need to eat something to keep your strength up."

CHAPTER TWENTY

Gail had a spring in her step after her evening at Lily's. Remembering how the evening ended gave her an extra bounce when she walked to the Ferry Building for lunch.

Suddenly, a bicycle courier swerved into her path. She was about to yell at the heavily tattooed young man for his clumsiness when he shoved a large envelope into her arms.

Fearing she had been given a bomb, Gail immediately dropped the envelope.

"Hey, lady, Jason is going to be supermad you refused his gift," the courier said.

"What?"

"I was paid to deliver that to you. You are Gail Joiner, right?"

"How do you know my name?"

"The guy who gave it to me told me. He said the package was important, so don't go throwing it away without looking at it."

Picking up the envelope, Gail glared at the courier. "Why didn't you come to my office and give it to me there?"

"He said not to."

"How on earth did you know who to deliver it to?" Looking around, Gail noted all the people who could have received the delivery by mistake.

"He gave me your picture and told me to wait. This is only my second day." The courier turned his bike around. "Oh, and don't call him unless you need something else."

"Do I owe you anything?"

"Nope. I get a cash bonus for finding you and a rush from the spy games. This delivery makes my month!"

Gail was left standing in the middle of the sidewalk as the young man peddled away. Glancing at the fruit and vegetable vendors around the entrance of the building, she decided to grab a flatbread sandwich and return to work to review what Jason had found.

Mission accomplished, Gail hurried back to her office. Closing the door behind her, she slit open the envelope and found twenty-five smaller envelopes inside. Each contained background information on one of the board members or one of the senior directors.

Jason had even highlighted the sections that would most interest her, like the debts owed by a couple of the board members who served on the committee that had given her the human resources metrics assignment.

While the information was not complimentary, nothing he'd uncovered seemed particularly illegal. Having saved Ken's envelope for last, she hoped to find a smoking gun.

The first page was his résumé. One of his jobs had been circled in red and an arrow pointed to the edge of the paper. Turning the sheet over, she saw a graph of ownership leading from Ken's past employer through several holding companies to Republic Beverage Distribution.

On page three of the printouts, she saw Ken's wife owned over a half million dollars of preferred stock in RBD. The information shocked Gail. She couldn't believe he thought they could get away with such blatant support of a rival business by putting it in his wife's name.

Republic had been a thorn in Tisane's side since its inception, but only in the past few months had they clashed openly. While the outrageous distribution charges in their contracts were annoying, their efforts to keep Tisane out of the middle of the country where the RBD truck fleet was based had been close to criminal. Nine months ago, RBD had made an offer to purchase Tisane and their network of suppliers, but Wan rebuffed any attempts to take control away from him.

Her heart heavy, she dialed Wan's direct line. "Wan, do you have time for me to come and chat with you? I'd like to bring Lily in with me, if possible."

"Sure, Gail. I'm free now," he said.

"Let me call her and see if she's available. I'll need about twenty minutes."

"No problem. I'm just doing paperwork while I wait for a conference call at seven o'clock when the Beijing office opens."

"Great. We'll be there as soon as we can." Gail disconnected the call and rang the warehouse. While one of Lily's assistant managers went to track her down, she collected everything Jason had sent her and put it in an interoffice envelope.

"Rush here," Lily answered the call at last.

"Hey, Lily. It's Gail. Would you be able to take a meeting with me and Wan?"

"Am I in trouble?"

"No, sweetie. It is about that thing we discussed. You know, about the thing?"

"That's as clear as mud, but I trust you will be more clear in person. I can shake loose in about ten minutes. Shall I meet you at your office or Wan's?"

"Wan's. And bring the stress ball the therapist gave you."

"Huh?"

"You're going to want to squeeze something painfully tight."

"Ah, boy. This is going to be a fun meeting."

"Just get up here when you can."

"Okay."

Gail hung up the phone, went to the scanner in the corner of her office, and quickly made a digital copy of everything. Carrying the CD and the paper copy, she made her way up to the president's office.

"Hey, Carla. I think he's expecting me," she said to the receptionist.

Carla nodded. "Yes, he is. Go on in."

Entering the corner office, Gail had to smile at the eager look on Wan's face. "You look like you're expecting good news."

His face fell. "Why else would you need to see me on such short notice?"

"I'm the HR director. I could have come in here for any number of negative reasons."

"Did you?"

"Yes and no. I decided to do some digging after I spoke to Lily the other day about the board. I involved a security consultant I know, but I need to warn you that nothing I'm about to show you can be used in a court of law."

"I don't recall authorizing any kind of investigation."

"I didn't ask for permission, and I think you're going to be in a very forgiving mood when you see what I have."

"I've found that much of what is useless to the courts can still be used to one's advantage." He sighed. "I might not like it, but I'll deal with it. Just tell me you didn't break any laws getting this stuff."

"I didn't and the search can't be traced back to us." Gail turned in her seat and smiled at Lily, who had tapped her cane against the door. "Hey, Lily. You're looking good."

"Thank you," Lily replied, coming into the room.

"No problem."

Carla stepped into the room carrying a clear glass teapot and three cups on a tray. Swaying gently inside the pot were four chrysanthemum flowers just beginning to unfurl in the hot water. "I figured you all needed something calming while you plot to take over the world."

"Thank you, Carla. You're a godsend!" Wan exclaimed.

Lily frowned. "There's no sugar."

"It is already sweetened. I added honey to the pot with the hot water."

After Carla poured out the first cups, she went back out and brought in an electric teakettle. "If anyone wants more, here's enough hot water for another pot."

"Thanks, Carla," Wan replied. He blew gently on the hot tea in his cup before lifting his eyes to Gail's. "Go on."

Gail handed the CD to Wan and the papers to Lily. "As I just told Wan, I did a little digging after our last conversation, Lily. I have a contact who will never be named. He found out some dirt on a few of the more aggressive board members, and something very interesting about Ken and his wife."

"Do tell."

"Yeah," Lily added. "Don't keep us in suspense."

"It looks like there might be enough dirt to blackmail those board members into acting against the best interest of the company. Unfortunately, there is no proof they are actually being blackmailed or even leaned on. They could be doing all this of their own free will."

Wan nodded. "Anything is possible, but I hate the idea that they are doing this out of greed."

"As for Ken, he not only used to be employed by a Republic subsidiary, but in his wife's name, owns a lot of stock in Republic itself."

"Really?" Wan asked. He opened the file and began scrolling through the pages. "Isn't that a clear conflict of interest?"

"No lawyer is going to accept these papers without an explanation." Gail shook her head. "We have to find other ways to prove it or other means to go after him."

Lily thumped her cane on the floor. "Just fire him! Use that damned at-will policy for good for once."

"We may be an at-will employer," Gail replied. "But he has a contract. Unless he is breaking the terms of his contract, it might be easier to pay the severance."

"No way," Lily said. "Don't give him a dime."

Wan nodded. "Now that we know what we're looking for, we should be able to discover this information independently."

"We can certainly try. It was found once, and knowing what to look for should make the search easier." Gail pointed toward the disc. "Basic banking and SEC searches should turn up the stock purchase."

"True," Wan agreed. "If he's bought this much stock and barely disguised his connection to it, he's overconfident. Chances are his arrogance has led him to do other things we can use against him."

"Like what?" Gail asked.

"Go over his employment agreement, résumé, and new hire documents. If there is a single date out of sequence or other error, I want it noted." Wan stood up and began pacing the room.

"I'm not sure what I'm going to find, but I will look," Gail promised.

Lily added, "Get one of your lawyers to hire a private detective."

"Oh, yes. I will call them immediately." Wan looked back at his desk. "I need a way to find out if any of the board members have been compromised."

"Do you have a solid board ally who can chat with them? Someone they might trust?"

Lily shook her head. "If it is greed driving this, better you find someone who seems willing to take a cut."

"You might be right." Wan acknowledged her point. "They might be willing to cut a co-conspirator in on a deal."

"I may be naïve," Gail interrupted, "but is there really that much of a payoff from what the board members are doing?"

"Manipulating stock prices is one thing, but our distribution setup is worth even more. Republic has never been able to break into either coast, so they've been restricted to domestic products they can get to market through rail or highways. We have an international network and contracts at two major West Coast and one East Coast port." Wan prowled his office. "Republic are bullies and I'll be damned if I'll let them run me out of business."

Gail was amazed at the transformation brought on by his fury. Instead of looking pale and defeated, he seemed energized and determined.

"They can't get away with it, can they?" Lily asked.

Wan rubbed his hands together. "Oh, no. Now that I know who my enemies are, I can take the battle to them."

Lily twirled her cane. "What are you going to do?"

"Contact every ally I have. Not just on the board, but in the industry. We'll marshal support and stop the takeover." Wan grinned. "As for Ken, if he's lucky, he won't go to jail."

"Excuse me?"

"I want you to look over all his hiring documents," he answered Gail. "If we can catch him in the slightest lie or misrepresentation…"

"We can fire him."

"Even better. We can charge him with fraud and put his ass away." Wan pointed at the door. "Find me some good news to break his contract and I'll work on saving my company from his cohorts."

"On it, boss!" Gail answered.

Wan and Lily laughed at her exuberance.

Drinking the last of her tea, Gail grinned. "What can I say? I respond well to authority."

"Indeed?" Wan raised an eyebrow, and then giggled when Gail and Lily blushed. "You guys are too cute for words. Okay, we know what needs doing, so let's do it. Just to be safe, let's keep this offline. No e-mails and leave any messages for me with Carla."

"No problem," Lily said.

"Yeah, I understand," Gail echoed. She nodded at Lily and walked back to her office with a far lighter step and a much lighter heart than she had just an hour before.

CHAPTER TWENTY-ONE

Lily's knuckles had barely touched the wood of Gail's front door before the door swung wide open. The sight of Gail in a tight black cocktail dress was enough to freeze her in place.

They stared in silence at each other before Lily blurted, "Wow. You clean up real good."

Gail blushed and ushered her inside. "You hush."

"No, you hush."

She and Lily hushed each other and laughed about it until Sierra skidded into the hallway.

"Hello," Sierra said.

"Wow!"

"Hey, that's what you said to me," Gail pouted.

"Well, I meant it then and I mean it now." Lily stepped forward and handed Gail a single peach-colored rose. "You both look lovely."

"Thank you. And for this beautiful thing, as well. Why don't you tell me what it means while I put it in some water?"

"Oh, it isn't much. A peach rose means gratitude and appreciation." Lily blushed. "And...um...it also means desire."

Gail smiled radiantly. "Then I want to thank you very much, both for the flower and the tickets. Sierra and I are really looking forward to the show."

"Have you ever been to Cirque du Soleil?"

Gail and Sierra shook their heads.

"It is supercool," Lily said. "You have no idea what the human body can do until you see their performers."

"Have you seen *Kooza*?" Gail asked.

"No. I've seen *Alegria* and *Dralion*." Lily raised her hands in the air. "Amazing. Absolutely wild and completely different. I'm totally stoked about this one."

"Ready to go?"

"Yeah. I appreciate you driving."

"No problem," Gail replied as she led the way to the car. "I prefer it actually."

"Oh, so you've got to be in control?"

"To some degree." Gail glanced sideways at Lily. "Although I have to admit there is pleasure to be found in letting go occasionally."

"That's good to know. I'm a fan of power exchanges myself."

"Hello? Impressionable minors present," called Sierra as she climbed into the backseat.

"Do you even understand what we're talking about?" Gail asked.

Sierra answered, "No, but when adults' voices sound like that, it is probably sex they're talking about."

"Sorry, kiddo. You'll just have to deal with it."

"Well, I might be more able to handle it if cotton candy was involved."

Lily turned around in her seat. "You want me to bribe you?"

"That's such a crude way of putting it."

Laughing, Lily said, "There will be cotton candy for all of us."

Lily, Gail and Sierra made their way through the crowds around PacBell Park and found their seats under the big tent. For the next three hours, they were transfixed by the haunting music, elaborate costumes and wondrous displays of acrobatics and imagination.

Sierra's eyes shone as she skipped toward the car after the show. "Oh, man. I want to be a trapeze artist. Or maybe a juggler."

Lily grinned at her exuberance. "You don't want to do the unicycle?"

"No. The others were more cool."

"Yeah, they did manage to make it seem effortless, don't they?" Gail tugged on her daughter's hand to calm her down. "A tremendous amount of work goes into each of those acts. You've got to start when you're young and work every day. Remember how much hard work it was when you were taking dance?"

Sierra scowled. "But I didn't like that."

"Being an acrobat is even harder than being a ballerina."

"And you have even less chance of making a living at it," Lily muttered.

Gail glared at her. "That's not the point." She turned back to Sierra. "The point is, if you're willing to make the commitment, I'll look into circus school."

Sierra sighed. "I'm already busy enough with soccer and normal school. I don't think I can add anything more."

"I'm proud of you for thinking it through. You're one smart cookie, and besides, you'd look funny in that rat costume."

"Thanks a lot."

"*De nada.*"

After the excitement of the show, it seemed to take forever to get the car out of the parking lot and onto the streets heading home. Lily kept moving around in her seat.

Gail turned to look at her when they were stopped at a traffic light. "You've overdone it," she said softly.

"No, I haven't." Lily shifted slightly.

"You can hardly sit still."

"It's been a long night."

"Why don't you come home with us?"

Lily frowned. "Are we…are you ready for this?"

"With your back like that, we're not going to do anything too acrobatic." Gail patted Lily's knee.

"Then what would happen if I went home with you?"

"I could give you a rubdown. I bet a massage would feel good, wouldn't it?"

"I'll be okay."

"I don't question that. I asked if you wanted a massage."

Drumming her fingers on the car door, Lily tried to think about what she really wanted. Finally, she nodded. "That would be nice."

"Good." Gail carefully navigated the vehicle home. Once they arrived, she put her daughter to bed and smiled when Lily wished Sierra good night.

Lily hesitated outside of Sierra's room.

"It's okay." Gail smiled at her. "Trust me." Holding out her hand, she took Lily's.

In the bedroom, she let go of Lily's hand and toed off her shoes before slipping off her dress. She smiled at Lily's suddenly wide-open eyes. "In case you were wondering, I'm leaving on the bra and panties. I just want a little more range of motion than that dress allows."

"Um, that's good," Lily replied as she kicked off her shoes and eased her pants off. Settling down on the bed on her stomach, she sighed at the feel of the cool sheets on her cheek.

Gail put a knee on the bed and tugged Lily's shirt up. Straddling her legs, she cracked her knuckles and began to work on Lily's upper back.

The knots let go one by one. Lily slowly drifted toward sleep. When Gail moved her attention to her lower back, she winced and murmured.

"Sweetie, do you need a pain pill?" Gail asked.

"It's not too bad."

"I can feel heat radiating off your spine."

"Fine. I'll take something." Lily moved her legs.

"No, I'll switch to the arnica cream and bring you a pill. You want naproxen or acetaminophen?"

"Whatever you have is fine."

"I have both or I wouldn't have offered. I'll get you a Tylenol 3." Getting up, Gail went into the bathroom. When she returned, she noticed Lily's stare. "What?"

"Why are you so nice to me?" Lily asked after swallowing the pill.

"Because I lo…um…I like you and I don't want to see people I like in pain."

Lily remained silent while Gail's magic fingers worked on her back. "When did you know?" she finally asked.

"Know that I liked you or that you liked me back?"

"The second."

"When you called me after you arrived home from the rehab center."

"But I never said anything then."

"You didn't have to. Your actions spoke for you."

Lily's speech slowed as she relaxed. "My friends know I like you a lot."

"Don't I know it!"

"What do you mean?"

"I had to sit through The Talk."

"What talk?"

"Your team cornered me at your party to ask me about my intentions to you."

"Those busybodies!"

Gail soothed Lily with her hands and her tone. "They care about you and don't want you hurt."

"They didn't have the right."

"Deal with it, sweetheart. Friends have a great deal of rights."

Lily had begun drifting off with the help of the painkiller and the healing touch of Gail's fingers. She purred a little and rubbed her cheek on Gail's sheets. "Mmm," she mumbled.

"What?" Gail asked quietly. She couldn't help smiling at the sight of Lily burying her nose in the pillow.

"Smells good."

"Oh?"

"Like Gail," Lily confided, half-asleep. "I like the way she smells."

"Just perfect," Gail said with a laugh. "I get you in my bed all loose and compliant and you fall asleep on me."

Feeling safe and loved, Lily let herself drift off.

CHAPTER TWENTY-TWO

"Shh!" Gail hissed.

"What's up, Mom," Sierra responded, dropping her gear bag by the front door.

"I'm trying to let Lily sleep in, so I need you to stop stomping around like a herd of elephants."

"Sorry!"

"And try to whisper," Gail admonished.

"Okay."

Shaking her head at the barely diminished decibels of Sierra's response, she herded her daughter into the car. She dropped off Sierra and her soccer gear at one of her teammates' homes, and then ran by Lily's house to pick up Butch. The dog happily sat in the front seat while she made a stop for some bagels and a collection of Sunday newspapers. Returning home, she carried everything up to her bedroom.

Sliding off her shoes, she paused and stared at the sleeping woman in her bed.

"Huh? What's up?" Lily blurted, half sitting up before slumping down on her back. "You smell like outside."

"It's a pretty foggy day."

"What were you doing?"

"Sierra has practice with her travel team, and I had to get her to the carpool."

"You don't want to take her yourself?"

"Me and the other soccer moms take turns driving to practices. It is just easier this way." Gail climbed back into bed. "Although it would be great if you could come to some of Sierra's games."

"I'd like that." Lily lifted her head and sniffed the air. "I smell dog."

"That's because I also picked up your pooch. I hope you don't mind me letting myself into your house."

"Naw, that's terrific." Lily reached her hand down for it to be licked by Butch. "I'm glad you thought of her."

"She's your baby. I won't ever forget what she means to you."

Lily rolled over and nestled against Gail's side. "I smell something else good too."

"That's because I got us breakfast." She lifted the paper bag from Noah's. "I stopped off to get some bagels and coffee."

"Yum." Lily wiggled closer until a large crinkling sound erupted. "What's that?"

"A few of the papers." Gail riffled through them. "I've got the *New York Times*, the *Washington Post*, the *LA Times*, and the *Chronicle*."

"Wow."

"It is a tradition of mine to read all the Sunday papers in bed, even if I have to get up, get them, and then get back into bed."

Lily accepted a paper and a bagel with cream cheese schmear. "Thanks for letting me be a part of your routine."

"I hope this is the first of many breakfasts in bed."

"Really?"

"Yeah, I've been thinking about what I want."

Lily looked at her. "Well? Are you going to tell me?"

"There are things I want in general and some things I want with you. Which do you want to hear first?"

After thinking for a moment, Lily said, "In general first."

"I want to never again volunteer to work overtime because I can't stand to be away from my partner for one second longer than I have to be. I want to be the center of someone's universe and I want them to be the center of mine."

"Okay." Lily plucked at the bedsheet.

"Now ask me the rest of the question."

"Um…what do you want from me?"

"The simple answer is that I want all of you. The good, the bad, your past, your future. I want to share the smallest details and the biggest issues with you."

"I haven't—"

Gail placed her fingers on Lily's lips. "This will be new to us both. I don't expect you to respond right away. I just want you to know that I want a future that has you in it." Spreading open the *Washington Post*, she focused on the newsprint.

***

Lily took another bite of her bagel and thought about her feelings for Gail.

She knew she had very strong, positive emotions toward Gail. But did she feel respect, gratitude, or even just affection?

During her recovery, a genuine friendship had developed between the two of them. As she came to know Gail better and more deeply, she realized there was a difference between what she felt for Gail and what she had experienced in the past.

She had enjoyed many passionate relationships where the chemical connection outweighed all rational thought or behavior. These brief connections had never been enough and they had never lasted. She knew now that she wanted something beyond the physical.

She thought she might have found that something more with Gail. Swallowing her last bite, she reached over and plucked the comics out of Gail's hands.

"Hey!" Gail cried indignantly.

Lily took hold of Gail's hand before she could grab the paper. "If we're going to do this, you need to know one thing."

"Oh?"

"I always read the funny pages first."

CHAPTER TWENTY-THREE

Jane Joiner skipped up the stairs of her daughter's house and nearly tripped over the large pickle jar sitting on the top step. The liquid inside was light brown from the four tea bags that had been steeping in the sunlight.

Picking up the jar, she knocked on the front door. When no one answered, she pulled out her set of keys and let herself in. "Hello," she called as she walked inside. "Gail, honey?"

She walked toward the sound of yelling and banging pots, stepped into the kitchen, and entered one of the circles of Hell. Heat rolled off the oven and every burner on the stove was boiling something. Hot water ran over the dishes piled high in the sink. "Goodness gracious."

"Mom! I didn't hear you knock," Gail said.

"Obviously, my dear." Jane pushed a stack of dirty bowls out the way and set the jar on the newly cleared space on the counter. "I brought in your sun tea."

Clearly distracted, Gail picked up a spoon to stir a pot before noticing the utensil had been used and tossing it into the sink. "Okay. Thanks."

"What in the world is going on?" Jane waved her hand. "I thought you were having someone special over to dinner, not throwing a party."

"It's not a party. I'm just not sure what she'd like, so I made... uh...a lot."

"So I see."

"I think I might have gone a little overboard." Gail turned to Sierra standing in the doorway. "Don't just stand there, make sure the picture frames are dusted."

Jane asked Sierra, "Has she been like this all night?"

"Worse," Sierra said, rolling her eyes. "She made me clean my closet and behind the toilets."

Glaring, Gail tossed the spoon into the sink and opened the oven to give the chicken a quick baste from the pan juices. "I don't know why you two think this is funny. Is it a crime to want things to be perfect for the first meal I've cooked for her?"

"We're not laughing, dear heart." Jane stepped forward and kissed Gail on the cheek. "Is there anything I can do?"

"Take the kid and get out of here."

"Thanks, Mom. Don't I feel special?"

"I didn't mean it like that. I've just got so much to do before she gets here."

"Is this the first time she's been to your house?" asked Jane.

"No. She's here pretty regularly now that she can navigate the stairs."

"And this is your first date?"

"No. We've gone out several times." Gail smirked. "We've even stayed in for a few."

"Then why are you driving yourself crazy?"

"I want things to be perfect for her."

"Just go up to your room, fix your hair and change your clothes," Jane said.

Gail looked frantically around the kitchen. "But..."

"Trust me on this. If you look nice, nothing else is going to matter." Jane began backing out of the kitchen. "Come on, Sierra. Let's leave your mother to it."

"All right."

"Make sure you have your homework and all you need for school tomorrow," Gail reminded her.

"I've got everything. God, why don't you ever listen?"

"Maybe because I don't think you're listening to me." Gail kissed Sierra on the forehead. "Mind your grandma. Thank you for agreeing to spend the night at her house tonight."

Sierra blushed. "Whatever. It wasn't anything."

"It means a lot to me. I love you, baby."

"Love you more."

"Love you infinity."

"I love you infinity plus one."

"Brat." Gail smiled, her mood seemingly improved by the banter. "Have a good night," she said to Jane.

"You too, dear. I'd say don't do anything I wouldn't do, but that would leave you with little to do."

"Bye, Mom." Gail pointed at the door. "Get out now."

Jane waved goodbye and led Sierra out the door, chuckling at the lengths Gail was going through to catch someone who seemed already caught.

***

Left alone, Gail turned down the heat on the various pots on the stove and shoved dishes into the dishwasher. She took off the apron and went upstairs to do what she could to follow her mother's advice about making herself look good.

She was blending two tones of eye shadow on her upper lid when the doorbell rang. Tossing the container into the sink, she smoothed down her blouse and headed to the door, opening it with, "Hey."

"Hello. You look beautiful," Lily said, thrusting a small bouquet of gardenias at her.

"Thank you. Why don't you come in?"

Lily brushed past her, blushing. "Something smells amazing."

"The flowers certainly do," Gail said, a flush heating her cheeks.

"I was thinking of dinner," Lily replied.

Despite the nerves Gail had experienced before Lily arrived, dinner went off without a hitch. After enjoying a three-course meal and the dessert that followed, she and Lily settled onto the couch for a bit of cuddling.

They kissed, laughed and shared stories from their pasts. Gail told the story about Sierra and her mother teasing her. Once they both stopped laughing, she asked a question that had been bothering her. "Do you ever think about your mom?"

"Not that it does any good, but I think about her all the time," Lily replied.

"Do you hate her?"

"Not anymore. I did once. I think my anger and hate was necessary to sustain me through those first really hard years. I wouldn't wish living on the streets to my worst enemy, so I still don't understand how someone who said she loved me could make me do it."

"Have you ever thought of contacting her again?"

"I did try. When I got my first real job, I still wasn't making enough to support myself. I went to my parents' place to see if they would co-sign on an apartment application." Lily sighed. "She wouldn't even open the door. She just looked at me through the glass. That's when I knew for sure that she agreed with my dad's decision to throw me out."

After a long pause, Gail wiped away a tear and whispered, "That is so sad."

"Yeah. I tried again on the ten-year anniversary of the fight. I was going to school again, I had a good job. I wanted to let them see that I was a success. Mom asked me if I was still a lesbian. When I said yes, she told me to leave. That nothing I did would ever make up for my mortal sin and the stain on my immortal soul."

"How could she be so cold?"

"I don't know. I remember how she acted when I was a child. She seemed so warm and affectionate. I think that's why it hurt so badly. I just could not understand how someone who supposedly loved me could do and say what she did."

"I'm sorry, sweetheart. Thank you for telling me."

Lily turned her head a little, facing Gail. "You know, telling you wasn't so bad."

"I'm glad."

"No, I mean it. I've never talked about this before."

"A burden shared is a burden halved."

"It feels like it. Thank you."

Gail cleared her throat. "Have your other partners asked, or have you just not volunteered?" she asked.

"I don't know. I guess maybe I acted like I didn't want to talk about it and no one pushed."

"Do you mind that I asked? I didn't think you were ever going to talk about it on your own."

Lily laughed. "You're probably right."

"Sometimes, the only way we're going to learn about each other is to ask some hard questions. You can always tell me you don't want to talk about something, but I'd appreciate it if you'd share."

"I'll try. You certainly make the process a lot less painful than I expected."

"Good." Gail paused. "Maybe we should try for another?"

Lily growled, "Don't push your luck."

Gail's laughter turned into another kiss. Together, they savored their joy, more so because of all the pain preceding it. As they kissed, Gail thought back over the things Lily had said. Making a decision, she pulled Lily up from the couch.

"Come with me," she said as she led her to the bedroom. Gail let go of Lily's hand when they reached the center of the room. Stepping back, she slowly removed all of her clothes.

Shaking her head when Lily began to follow suit, Gail stepped closer. "My turn," she murmured, brushing Lily's hands aside. "Please let me take care of you."

Wordlessly, Lily let her arms drop to her side. She stood still while Gail carefully undressed her, kissing every inch of skin as it was revealed. When they were both naked, Gail gathered Lily into her arms and held her close. Stroking her hair, Gail began whispering to her, telling her how beautiful she was, how strong, how loving.

Twisting, Lily struggled in her grasp. Gail was stronger than she looked. She kept caressing Lily and talking softly until her resistance melted. She spoke to Lily about the flecks of green and gold in the brown of her eyes, the dimple on her cheek that only showed when she smiled, the play of muscles when she moved— all of the things that she loved about her.

It wasn't long before Lily was weeping. Silent tears poured from her eyes as Gail spoke of how marvelous she was, how much Sierra loved her, and how much she meant to her. Gail's voice was thick with emotion when she described the sadness she felt when Lily shared the story of her past, and how honored she was to be trusted with Lily's precious heart.

Gail eased her down upon the bed and kept up the barely there touches. Tenderly, she used her hands and lips to show Lily her love. The body beneath hers began trembling, but she kept massaging her gently, never breaking contact with the soft, scarred skin.

Taking a pillow, Gail eased it under Lily's lower back and encouraged her to bend her knees and open her legs.

"Gail?"

"Please, Lily. Let me love you." Gail nearly begged, and then nearly wept herself when Lily acquiesced. She tried to keep her hunger from her face, but even so, Lily's entire body blossomed with color as she physically reacted to the weight of Gail's gaze.

Nestling between the open legs, Gail massaged Lily's stomach and inner thighs. She smelled the rich scent of Lily's arousal, but she wouldn't be rushed toward completion. Focusing on Lily's labia, she massaged each of her lower lips before delicately circling a finger around and across her clitoris.

"Oh!"

"Shh, Lily. Just breathe and let me love you," Gail instructed, using every breath and every touch to demonstrate how much she cherished her.

Moving her finger downward, she looked up into desire darkened eyes for permission before easing inside. She didn't thrust, but continued her massage, this time from inside, exploring

Lily until her finger made contact with her G-spot. More firmly, she pressed against the spongy surface before lowering her head to circle her tongue over Lily's clit.

Varying the depth and speed of her strokes, Gail moved her tongue in counterpoint until Lily was swept away by her climax.

For a long time afterward, Gail watched Lily sleep, seeing the remains of tears on her face and lashes and studying the curve of a smile on her lips. Despite her own arousal, she realized she was happy to just enjoy the contentment of the woman in her arms.

Snuggling against Lily, Gail joined her in smiling sleep.

CHAPTER TWENTY-FOUR

"Are you ready for the meeting?" Lily asked.

Wan pulled his suit jacket on and brushed at the fabric until it lay perfectly. "As ready as I'll ever be."

"Who's going to be there?"

"The whole board except for the international members. They'll be on webcams and teleconferencing in, though."

"How is this going to work?"

"I'm going to try and let the meeting run to see just how far the corruption goes." Wan picked up his briefcase. "Things are going to be tense. I need you to be silently supportive, no matter how angry you get."

"Are you sure I should be there?" Lily rubbed her damp palms on her pants. "I'm not the most diplomatic person on your staff."

"They're going to go after your department. You should be there in case I need you to supply some numbers." Wan smiled at her. "You're also my best friend, and I want you there watching my back."

"You know I'll back whatever play you make."

"Good. Let's do this thing." Wan led the way down the hall to the main conference room.

Board members filled fifteen of the seats at the table. The group was predominately Asian with a few aging hippies and several Europeans. Sitting directly behind the board chairman was Ken Williams. He smirked at Lily when she took her seat behind Wan.

"We have some serious issues to discuss at this emergency meeting of the board," Chairman Denham Mitchell stated after calling the meeting to order. Lily knew he was only a couple of months older than Wan, but his thinning hair and sallow skin made him look a decade older. "We're about to close the quarter, and the reports from distribution are not only disappointing, they're unacceptable."

Pieter Shalnova, president of the Russian tea consortium and one of Wan's closest friends on the board, spoke up. "There were mitigating factors for the shortfall."

Mitchell ignored the interruption. "Additionally, distribution exceeded their operational budget by five hundred thousand dollars."

Lily clenched her hands tightly together and tried not to react.

"Most of those expenses are from the rebuild. The lawsuit will pay for those, not any individual department's budget," Wan responded mildly. "Strange, though, that the figures you have don't reflect the settlement numbers properly. One might think you were getting inside information instead of official accounting reports."

"A small discrepancy that matters little."

"I would think the sharing of confidential company data would be cause for concern for the board."

"Of course, if someone from outside the board had used this information, there would be an issue. I can assure you all that the information has been protected."

"But that doesn't answer who has seen it," Wan responded. "All of you in this room and all of my senior managements signed non-compete and non-disclosure agreements. I want to know who violated their agreement and on whose authorization it happened"

"The committees were given a lot of latitude to gather information."

"I've reviewed the minutes. There was never a directive to collect interim data." Wan opened his briefcase and pulled out a folder. "Oddly, these same erroneous figures appear in an internal memo from Republic that I received from a private investigator whom I hired. I hope everyone realizes that trade secret violations will be prosecuted to the fullest extent allowed by law."

The board members straightened in their seats and glanced at one another.

"I ask again, Chairman Mitchell, where did you get this information?" Wan asked.

Mitchell glanced over his shoulder into the wide eyes of the Vice President of Marketing, Ken Williams.

"Interesting," Wan noted. He pulled out another folder. "It might interest you to know that the private investigator submitted a report that Ken Williams used company property, resources and funds to further his personal ends. Further, his family owns and controls a five percent stake in Republic Distribution." Wan slid the folder down the table. "Thus putting him in direct violation of the conflict of interest agreement he signed upon his hiring."

The chairman spread his fingers on the folder. "I knew nothing about this. My concern was first and foremost for the growth of the company."

"The compound annual growth rate of Tisane Enterprises has never dipped below five percent. I have never given any of you cause for concern. On the other hand, I think the rest of the board should consider holding a vote of no confidence now on the chairman."

"I make a motion indicating the lack of confidence of the board in the current chairman, and should such a motion pass, call for the immediate removal of the chairman from office," Louise Yang, an importer of southern Chinese *pu'er* tea, immediately stated.

Wan leaned forward. "Denham, in consideration of our long professional relationship, I urge you to not make the board vote on this. If you resign, I will not have you prosecuted for your role in this affair. You will, of course, forfeit all stock options."

Mitchell shoved his chair back from the table and turned on Ken Williams. "I can't believe I listened to you!"

"No wait," Ken pleaded. "We can still do this. They are bluffing and wouldn't dare prosecute anyone. It would be a publicity nightmare."

"Don't be so sure, Ken. We can explain a lot with restructuring after the recent tragedy." Wan pulled out another folder. "In any event, you will be fired and charged with fraud. You lied on your résumé and provided false information on several of your new hire documents."

Ken jumped to his feet and stormed toward Lily. "You bitch!"

"Actually, the Human Resources department identified your dishonesty," Wan replied.

"So the real bitch is her girlfriend." Ken glared around the room. "How about a vote of no confidence in a CEO who allows two of his subordinates to engage in a homosexual relationship?"

"Honestly, Ken. Is that the best you can do?" Wan asked. "Have you forgotten that we're based in San Francisco? Not only do we have a pretty extensive nondiscrimination policy, we also don't have a policy against personal relationships except for direct reports. There are no violations by anyone here but you." Reaching over to the phone, he dialed his secretary. "Carla, please send security in here."

Lily sat back in her seat, relishing the drama of Ken being escorted out of the conference room. She was even happier when Wan indicated the meeting would take a ten-minute break and they could leave the room.

CHAPTER TWENTY-FIVE

Gail met Lily and Wan in the hallway outside the conference room. "You were amazing!" she exclaimed.

"You saw it?" Wan asked.

"Yeah, we were all watching the live feed downstairs."

"Thank you for everything." Wan grabbed her in a hug, and then shoved a bottle of Veuve Clicquot Brut into her hands. "This is cause for celebration. While I've got to make nice with the remaining board, you should take Lily home and enjoy the rest of the day off with my compliments."

"Thanks, Wan." Gail turned to Lily, "Shall we?"

"Sure. I wouldn't want to cross my boss. He's wicked powerful." Lily gave Wan a hug. "You rocked it, chief!"

"Thanks. Now get out of here." Wan picked up another two bottles of champagne from Carla's desk and walked back into the conference room.

Gail examined the bottle's orange label. "This looks good. You ready to pop the cork?"

"Sure. You want to give me a ride home?"

"Sounds perfect."

"Why don't we grab anything we need and meet at my car?"

Gail agreed and strode off to her office. She did not need much more than her laptop and to tell Chet her plans. "Wan has given us the afternoon off."

"You deserve it, boss. It was so good to see Ken get what was coming to him."

"That reminds me, would you pull up the job description for the VP position and squirt it to me with the contact information for the executive search company that found him? I want to give them a chance to make up for finding Ken."

"No problem."

With a wave, she left her office and went to her car. Gail drove to Lily's home where she waited impatiently while Lily let Butch out into the yard to do her business.

When Lily headed into the kitchen, Gail stopped her with a hand on her shoulder. "Take me to your bedroom."

"Don't we need glasses?"

"I'm not going to drink this champagne from a glass. We're celebrating more than just the survival of the company. We're celebrating yours as well."

"Um, okay." Lily followed Gail upstairs. "So we're drinking it from the bottle?"

"Not exactly." Popping the cork, Gail caught the overflow in her mouth. Once she swallowed, she grinned and said, "Get undressed and lay down on the bed." She watched avidly as Lily complied. "You don't mind if the sheets get a little messy, do you?"

"Depends on the mess."

"Turn over on your stomach." Once Lily complied, Gail tilted the champagne bottle over the middle of Lily's back. She heard Lily gasp at the first touch of the cool liquid.

"Oh!" Lily shivered as the champagne spread across her skin. "That's so strange. I can feel the bubbles!"

Gail watched while rivers of champagne formed puddles and pools. Setting the bottle on the nightstand, she bowed down to lap up the sparkling wine. "I can taste the bubbles," she whispered, savoring the sweetness of the wine and a slight saltiness of sweat from the day's exertion. Smacking her lips, she ran her hand across Lily's sides, pausing when her fingers moved over the scars. "You taste so good."

Lily moaned when Gail's tongue pressed firmly along her spine. She braced her arms on the mattress and pushed up. "I want to roll over," Lily whispered. "I want to touch you, too."

Their limbs entangled and their passion flashed brightly. Kisses became deeper. Gail fought to move on top of Lily, who grappled for dominance. After a few more heated kisses, Lily relaxed so Gail could roll them over.

Gail smiled down at Lily and kissed her gently. She moved her mouth lower, biting and licking Lily's neck. She mingled her kisses with intense sucking that would leave marks on Lily's skin. Her hands traveled the terrain of Lily's body, feeling her way over the hills and valleys of her curves. The scars were like roads on a map, and she followed them with one destination in mind. She paused before taking what was offered.

Lily's eyes opened and locked with Gail's. "Please," she whispered.

Gail teased the damp tendrils of hair between Lily's legs before sliding her finger across Lily's clit. "We have more champagne," she whispered. Grabbing the bottle, she slid down Lily's body, kissing and nipping as she moved. Finally settling between Lily's spread legs, she held the bottle over Lily's pussy. "Hold still. If you can."

"Oh, God," Lily murmured, staring at Gail. When the cool liquid splashed down, she moaned, "Sweet Jesus."

Lapping at the combination of fluids Gail smiled. "Sweet is right." She licked her lips. "I can't believe how good you taste."

The muscles in Lily's legs jumped as she visibly struggled to keep them open wide. "Gail, please. I need you."

"I know, sweetie." Gail blew a breath across the damp curls.

"I'm going to give you exactly what you need." She concentrated her attention on Lily's clit, kissing it gently.

Lily brought her knees up, opening herself even more. "Don't stop."

Humming, Gail ran her tongue along the puffy lips of Lily's labia. Returning to Lily's clitoris, she found a rhythm and poured all her affection into the task. She reached up to hold Lily's bucking hips until Lily brought her hands down and pushed her head gently away.

"Too much," Lily said.

"Never," Gail laughed. She sat up and took another sip of champagne. "Are you thirsty?" Taking another mouthful, but not swallowing, she leaned over Lily and kissed her before opening her lips and sharing the champagne.

"I'm thirsty for more than that." Lily moved between Gail's legs, spreading them wide before lowering her mouth to the tender folds of flesh, using her tongue and her teeth. She slid two fingers into Gail's pussy.

"Lils," Gail cried out. She clutched at the sheets, shuddering from the sensations created by the movements of Lily's mouth.

Lily left her fingers inside Gail, who squeezed them with her internal muscles. Lily crawled up to kiss her neck. As Gail's first orgasm passed, Lily began to move her fingers again. "Once is never enough, is it?"

Gail's breath quickened and she came again, nearly rising from the bed as the pleasure crashed through her. Finally, she reached down and pulled Lily's hand from between her legs to rest it between her breasts. Turning her head, she gazed in wonder at Lily before laughing softly.

"What's so funny?"

"The Bible says not to get drunk on wine as that leads to debauchery."

Lily reached over for the half-empty bottle of champagne. "We have plenty left and hours before Sierra comes home. There is more debauching to be done!"

"Well, then, fill me with your spirit!"

Gail and Lily proceeded to get very, very drunk on the champagne and each other.

Bella Books, Inc.

Women. Books. Even Better Together.

P.O. Box 10543
Tallahassee, FL 32302

Phone: 800-729-4992
www.bellabooks.com